Lina,
Get to know
Ricky!

OTHER BOOKS BY ERIC WALTERS

Ricky

ERIC WALTERS

HarperTrophyCanada™
An imprint of HarperCollinsPublishersLtd

HarperCollins Publishers Ltd
2 Bloor Street East, 20th Floor
Toronto, Ontario, Canada
M4W 1A8

www.harpercanada.com

National Library of Canada Cataloguing in Publication

Walters, Eric, 1957–
Ricky / Eric Walters. – Mass market pbk. ed.

ISBN 0-00-639225-3

I. Title.

PS8595.A598R52 2004   jC813'.54   C2003-905650-3

IMS 9 8 7 6

Printed and bound in the United States
Set in Dante

Chapter One

There was a heavy knock on the door and I could hear my dog Candy running toward it, barking and howling furiously. I knew without looking at my watch that it was eight-thirty and that the person pounding on the door was my best friend, Augie. I also knew that I still had a few more things to do before I'd be ready to leave for school, and that Augie wouldn't be happy about waiting.

"Coming!" I yelled down the stairs. It would have been faster and easier just to shout for him to come in, but Augie never wanted to walk in by himself. He was afraid of my dog. Actually, he was afraid of most of my animals. At least with the dog he had good reason. Candy was not particularly friendly to anybody. She was part collie, part beagle, part Lab and all mean.

I thundered down the steps, leaping down the last half dozen in one bound and landing at the bottom with a crash. I grabbed Candy by the collar and dragged her away from the front door and into the living room, pulling another door closed so she couldn't get back into the hallway.

"Come in," I called as I threw open the front door. "Sorry, I'll be ready in a few—"

"Minutes," Augie said.

"Yeah," I said. "I just have to—"

"Feed and check on a few more animals," Augie said, finishing my sentence again.

"Yeah . . . that's right," I said, nodding as I started back up the stairs. "How did you know that?"

"Big surprise," Augie said, following me. "It's not like I have to be a member of the psychic hotline to figure out what you were going to say."

He pressed himself against the far wall as he passed by the living room. It was like he was afraid Candy would somehow escape and get at him. She growled ominously through the closed door.

"Why doesn't that dog like me?" he asked.

"She doesn't like anybody except me and my sister and father. If you don't *live* here, she figures you shouldn't *be* here."

"It would be a lot easier if you just met me in front of your house. But that would mean you'd have to be ready on time every now and again."

"I have been ready on time *sometimes*," I said.

"You have? When?"

"I think it was the first day of school. Remember?"

"That was a long time ago," Augie said.

"Not that long ago. We've only been in school for five weeks."

"Six . . . not that I'm counting. And that leaves ten more weeks until Christmas break."

"Actually, it does sound like you're counting," I commented as I opened my bedroom door and Augie trailed in behind me. "School isn't *that* bad."

"Not bad for you—" Augie wrinkled up his nose as he entered. "The stink is too revolting . . . with so many animals in here," he said. "How many are there again?"

"That depends."

"Depends on what?"

I gestured to the large wooden box attached to the window. "I don't know how many of my squirrels are in their nest and how many are outside, and Candy's downstairs and my sister's cat is in her room, and of course my cats aren't allowed in the house so—"

"But how many would there be if they were all here?" Augie asked.

I shrugged. "Twenty-nine."

"I thought there were more."

I shook my head. "One dog, four cats, six squirrels, a rabbit, two hamsters, four rats, a gerbil, a grouse, two groundhogs, four iguanas, two budgies and, of course, the alligator."

"Of course . . . we wouldn't want to forget the alligator."

My alligator, Ollie, sat in its pen, a wooden box almost six feet long and three feet wide that took up

3

one whole end of my bedroom. Half of its home was filled with water and the other half with sand. Ollie was in the water right now, only his eyes and nostrils visible above the waterline.

He wasn't really even an alligator. He was a caiman, the South American cousin of the alligator, but when I said I had a caiman, people never knew what I was talking about.

There really isn't much different between the two in terms of appearance—you'd have to be an expert to tell them apart. The major difference is in the way they act. While nobody would ever call an alligator friendly, caiman tend to be downright nasty. I read somewhere that they are one of the few creatures in the world that kill for fun. Even if they aren't hungry they just kill things. That sounds awful, but of course one of the other animals that kills for no reason is man.

Augie stared at Ollie from across the room. It was the one animal I had that made him even more nervous than Candy.

"I don't even know why you have that thing. At least the cats and squirrels are cuddly," Augie said. "That thing gives me the creeps."

"There's nothing to worry about," I said.

What I wouldn't confess was that Ollie was starting to make me nervous, too. I didn't like to pick him up unless I had to.

"You have to admit that it's an interesting animal."

"Interesting, right . . . it's interesting the way it looks at me, like I'm its next meal," Augie said as he walked over and peered cautiously into Ollie's box.

"Don't be silly. He's less than three feet long. There's no way he could eat a fourteen-year-old . . . especially one as big as you."

"That's good to know," Augie offered as he looked down at the alligator, who was looking up at him.

"The worst he could do is jump up and take off a couple of fingers."

Augie straightened and stuffed his hands into the pockets of his pants—his new pants. Augie always had new clothes. Nice new clothes. His family owned and ran Levy's Department Store and they lived above the shop. So I guess it only made sense that he was always so well dressed. I was pretty sure he wore more new clothes every month than I even owned.

"We're going to be late," Augie said, glancing at his watch.

"We can still get there on time . . . if we boot it."

"I don't want to run. It gets me all sweaty. Girls don't like it if you're all sweaty."

I smiled to myself as I topped up the pellets in the gerbil cage. I was shocked it had taken so long for Augie to mention girls this morning. He always talked about girls. He always thought about girls. He told me he even dreamed about them. Personally, I thought they were . . . I don't know . . . okay, but it wasn't like the way

5

Augie thought about them, which was constantly. Maybe it had something to do with our ages. We were in the same grade but there was two years' difference between our ages. I'd skipped a grade and Augie had failed once.

Augie didn't ever do that great in school. What I didn't understand was *why* he didn't do well in school. He was probably—no, make that definitely—the smartest kid I knew. He knew things. Things about sports and news and people and buses and subways. When we went downtown on Saturdays, he always took the lead. He could find his way around the city better than I could get around the neighbourhood.

"I've just got to check on the squirrels," I said as I walked over to their nest.

It was another big wooden box, this one attached to my bedroom window. My father had made it and re-cut the glass so it would fit in the window. The squirrels could climb into the nest from the outside—and I could check on them by opening up the back. That meant they couldn't come into the house unless I invited them, but they had a safe place to sleep. My father was a carpenter, so he was pretty good at making things, and he also knew lots about animals. He said that this would be the closest thing we could make to the nest they used to share with their mother—before she was killed.

We'd found a dead squirrel out in front of our house

in the spring. My father said that he knew it was a mother with babies because most of the hair on her tail was missing. They pull the hair out to line their nests to keep the babies warm. It was awful thinking about those poor babies on their own in a tree someplace, waiting for their mother, and slowly starving to death.

That's when my father borrowed a ladder and we spent an entire day looking for the nest. He climbed up and down and I stood at the bottom holding the ladder. We finally found them—six tiny bundles of black fluff, all huddled together in one ball. He put them inside his coat, one at a time, carried them down and handed them to me.

At first they were so little that I didn't think any of them would live. But they did. They lapped up milk and ate Frosted Flakes and bread and an occasional peanut—and grew. They were almost big enough now to take care of themselves.

I undid the latch at the back of their nest, and the panel opened to reveal balled-up blankets containing a bundle of squirrels all rolled together. One of them opened an eye and then a second stretched, and within a few seconds they all started to wiggle around.

"Here you go, guys, breakfast in bed," I said as I poured in a serving of cereal and dried bread.

"They are cute," Augie said. "That was so cool when you took them in to show to the class last year."

That was only a few weeks after I'd originally found

them, and I brought them in to show to our science teacher, Mr. Johnston.

"The girls loved them," Augie said. "Girls love squirrels."

"It's funny," I said. "Squirrels they like and rats they hate. And if you think about it, the only difference between the two is that squirrels have fancy tails."

I pushed the panel back into place, leaving the squirrels free to go outside but not to come into my room. "Okay, I'm ready, let's get going," I said.

"About time."

I took a last look back into my room before I closed the door behind me. I was positive they'd all be okay for the day . . . well, almost positive. Maybe I should just go back and check one more time. I hesitated at the top of the steps.

"Come on or I'm going without you!" Augie yelled up the stairs.

I started after him. "I'll meet you on the porch. I have to let Candy loose."

Augie headed out, anxious to get some distance between him and my dog. As I opened the living room door, Candy scrambled past and rushed after Augie, snapping and snarling. I quickly ran into the kitchen and checked that all the stove burners were turned off and that the toaster was unplugged. Next I stopped and made sure the back door was locked. I took my lunch off the counter—I'd made it first thing this morning—

and rushed to the hall, grabbing my coat and backpack. I put both my lunch and my coat inside the pack and slung it on my back.

Now, was there anything else I needed to remember? Stove . . . toaster . . . taps all turned off . . . lunch . . . school stuff . . . key? I reached up and took hold of the chain hanging around my neck. Attached to it was the key I'd need to let myself back in at the end of the day.

"Take care of the place, girl," I said to Candy as I reached down and gave her a final pat on the head. I clicked the lock on as I squeezed out the door.

Chapter Two

Augie had already left the porch and was halfway down to the sidewalk. I hurried after him.

"This is even later than usual," Augie said. "Maybe *you* can afford a trip to the office, but if I'm sent down there one more time I'm in big trouble."

I absently nodded in agreement. I wasn't really listening. Instead, I was wondering . . . did I lock the door? Did it click in or did I accidently leave the door un—

"It's locked!" Augie hollered, startling me out of my thoughts.

"I know . . . I'm almost positive it's locked."

"I am positive!" Augie said. "I heard it click!"

"You did?"

That was reassuring . . . but he had been almost to the sidewalk and there was no way he could have heard it. I hesitated, and Augie drew away from me a few steps as he kept up his pace.

"You don't have to check," he said.

He was right, of course. I didn't have to check. It was locked, the way it was always already locked when I went back to make sure every morning. But if I didn't double-check I'd be thinking about it all day.

"I'll be right back," I called over my shoulder as I turned and ran back toward my house.

"I'm not waiting!"

"I'll catch up!" I shouted without looking back.

I sprinted down the street. Thank goodness I was only a couple of dozen houses away from my place. I cut across my front lawn, leaped up the stairs to the porch and skidded to a stop in front of the door. I jiggled the handle. It was locked . . . like always. I heaved a sigh of relief and then, not having time to savour the moment, spun back around and ran to catch Augie.

I could see him up ahead, at the end of the street. He was sitting on top of a mailbox, waiting, the way he *always* waited after he *always* told me he wouldn't wait, after I *always* ran back to check my door.

"Thanks," I panted out.

He jumped down. "What choice did I have?" he asked with a shrug. "If I didn't walk with you, I don't think you could find your way to school."

"Of course I could find my way to . . ." I didn't finish the sentence. "Thanks for waiting for me."

"Save your breath . . . you'll need it if you want to be there on time. Let's go!"

He started to run and I started after him. I was already short of breath from my run back to the house, but there was no way I wasn't going to keep up with him. We crossed the first street, dodging the cars as they passed. Augie was half a dozen paces ahead of me. I tried to close the gap, but each time I picked up my pace, he increased his to match. We kept running, the whole length of the block, then crossed the next street and continued along the next. I wanted to call out, to ask him to slow down, but I didn't. It was important to keep up with him. My lungs started to ache. I stared right at the middle of Augie's back, not looking left or right or up or down. Just focusing on Augie, not letting him get away.

"Okay," Augie said as he slowed down a bit. "We'll be on time now."

"Are . . . you . . . sure." I gasped as I caught up.

"Positive. Look."

There were kids up ahead, kids from our school, walking. Some were by themselves and others were in little groups. Nobody seemed in any rush, so it was safe to assume none of us was going to be late.

"Do you see what I see?" Augie asked.

"Depends on what you see."

"Sylvia and Carol?" Augie asked.

I nodded. They were two girls we'd known for a long time, from our old school, General Mercer. It only went to grade six, so last year we'd started off at the middle school, Osler Senior Public, along with all the kids from seven other elementary schools.

"Do you want to join them?"

I shook my head. "Not really."

"Why not?"

"I don't know . . . I just . . ."

"They like you, you know."

I felt myself blush. "I don't know about that, but they do like you."

"Of course they do. What's not to like? All the girls love me."

I knew that he was exaggerating, and bragging, but really not much of either. Almost all the girls in the school did like him. He was the best athlete in the whole school, and he was always friendly to everybody. And besides that, he was also funny.

Augie always had jokes to tell, and he did these incredible imitations. He could sound just like some famous people, and cartoon characters, and even teachers. He did an impression of our principal that was just about perfect.

"Let's talk to them. You need the practice."

"What do you mean?" I asked.

"Practice. It's no different than playing basketball. The way to get better at anything is to do it more. You need to talk to girls more."

"But—"

"No buts. Let's catch up to them. You need to learn to talk to girls if you want to get anywhere in life."

"I don't need to talk to girls to get where I want to be. All a vet needs is to understand animals."

"And I suppose these animals are just going to come wandering in by themselves," Augie said.

"Of course not. Their owners will bring them in to see me and—"

"And those owners . . . would they happen to be people . . . some of whom might be girls?"

I sighed deeply. I knew there was no way to beat Augie in an argument. What I needed to do was change the direction.

"I guess we can talk to them," I said.

"That's more like it."

"I just thought you wouldn't want to."

"Me?" Augie sounded genuinely shocked. "Why wouldn't I want to talk to girls?"

"I just thought you'd want to wait a little . . . you know, until you weren't sweating so much."

"Sweating?" Augie reached up and wiped his forehead. "Jeez! I told you that would happen if we had to run so hard!"

Actually, I couldn't tell if he was sweating. The important thing was that he *believed* he was.

"You'll have to wait till later to practise talking to girls," he said. "Besides, you've already had enough practice today."

"I have?"

"Sure, the running."

"How's that practice?" I asked.

"Practice for the basketball tryouts that are coming

up. That run will help get you into good enough shape to make the team."

"I'm a lock for the team," I said smugly.

"I wouldn't be so sure about that. There're lots of good players in grade eight."

"Yeah, but that's not my problem. I only have to worry about the kids in grade seven."

"You don't have to worry about any of the seveners," Augie said. "None of them are trying out for the senior team."

"And neither am I. I'm going out for the junior team."

"The junior team is for juniors."

"I know I'm a senior, but I also know I'm the same age as the grade sevens and that means I can try out for that team."

"You could, but do you really want to? You could make the senior team. It's the same guys from last year's junior team, and you were on the team when you were only supposed to be in grade six," Augie reasoned.

"You're right, I could make the team, but I want to do more than that."

"Now I don't understand what you mean," Augie said.

"I was on the team last year, but I didn't get that much playing time."

Augie shrugged. "It's just that some of the other players are—"

"Better and bigger than me. And it seems like every-body has gotten even bigger over the summer."

"Some of us have grown," Augie said, patting me on the head and grinning.

"I've grown!" I snapped. "Just not as much as you . . . but then again, I'm not nearly as old as you."

My words wiped the grin off Augie's face, and I instantly regretted what I'd said. He was pretty sensitive about being older than everybody else. Almost as sensitive as I was about being the youngest. And it was getting worse.

Everybody else did seem to be growing faster than me. There was a time when I actually was pretty tall, but now more than half the boys and two-thirds of the girls were taller than me. And some of the boys had scraggly whiskers starting to grow on their upper lips and voices that were starting to change. And the girls . . . some of them were . . . developing. If I was nervous around them before, now I was downright terrified.

"You know, playing on the junior basketball team will not impress one single girl in all of grade eight," Augie said.

I was relieved he'd started talking to me again. I really hadn't meant to hurt his feelings.

"Maybe I don't want to impress any girls in grade eight."

"Impressing girls is half the reason to play basket-ball," Augie said. "Being on the junior team, the only girls you'll impress are seveners . . ." Augie stopped and spun me around by the shoulder. "Say, is that your game? You'd be the only grade eight on the team and every girl in grade seven would be impressed by you. Right? You could have your pick of the girls in grade seven."

"I don't want my pick of the girls. I just like playing basketball! Does everything with you have to be about girls?" I demanded.

A thoughtful look came over Augie's face. "Well . . . yes."

"Ugh! You're hopeless!" I said.

Augie smiled. "You shouldn't be calling me hopeless, little buddy," he said, in a perfect imitation of Yogi the Bear. "If you're not nice I won't be sharing any of my *pic-i-nic* baskets with you. Okay, Boo-Boo?"

I shook my head. It was impossible to stay mad at Augie. "Okay, Yogi," I answered back, trying my best to sound like Boo-Boo.

"That's more like it. Do you want to take the short-cut?"

"No," I said, shaking my head vigorously. Augie was referring to an alley that cut down behind the stores and then came in behind the school. There was a hole in the fence where you could get into the schoolyard. The route was almost two blocks shorter that way.

"It would save us some time," Augie said.

"Or get us killed."

"Nobody's been killed going that way."

"Maybe not killed, but I hear the stories."

There was a high school four blocks over, and the high school students hung around in the alley in the morning before school and then again after school every day. They'd taken to "charging" people—mostly kids in our school who were younger and smaller—to let them pass by. Some kids lost their lunch money. A couple who put up a fight or argued had been roughed up. You had to be stupid to go that way.

"We'll just cut through . . . don't worry. Don't I always take care of you?" Augie asked.

"And who's going to take care of you? You're a big kid here at Osler, but you're not so big compared to high school kids. Besides, I thought we were going to catch up to Carol and Sylvia," I said, motioning ahead.

"But . . ."

"I can't see any more sweat on your face," I said. Not that I ever had. I was worried about talking to the girls, but I was downright scared of going through that alley.

Augie smiled. "You know I was just kidding about going through the alley. Hey, girls!" he yelled, and they turned around. "Wait up for us!"

I shook my head. And I'd thought I was fooling him.

Chapter Three

The snake's tongue darted out—not once, not twice, but three times. It was testing, smelling, letting the scent that was wafting through the air tell it which route was best. Decided, in gentle undulations it moved forward. Brown skin with a brilliant pattern of shifting black diamonds, it glistened and shone in the bright light. Smooth and graceful and silent. Amazing how soundlessly an animal that large could travel. From nose to tail it was almost two metres in length. Long, but not long at all for a boa constrictor. Someday it would be almost three times that size.

Up ahead there were twenty—no twenty-five—animals . . . a herd. They sat, unmoving and unaware of the danger. The snake froze as one of the animals shifted and turned, not looking quite in its direction, but close. Not moving, partially hidden behind cover, the snake hadn't been seen. It was essential to remain undetected. It wasn't as fast as its prey, and if the herd saw it, they would startle and be lost. Stealth was needed to close the gap. Then, when close enough, it would throw its coils.

At that moment stealth would be replaced by strength. Sheer strength. Strength to tighten its coils around the animal, squeezing tighter and tighter each time it took a breath or contracted a muscle . . . until the animal was helpless, unable to move . . . and then unable to breathe . . . finally lapsing into unconsciousness . . . to be eaten alive . . . swallowed whole. The jaws hinging open to eat a prey that was many, many times bigger than the snake was wide.

Imagine the terror of an animal caught within those deadly coils, knowing that it could not escape, knowing that its death would come soon, that it would be squeezed into unconsciousness and then eaten . . . alive!

The boa came forward, now moving even more slowly . . . closing the gap . . . four feet . . . three feet . . . still too far to strike . . . two feet . . . and then—

"Mr. Johnston!" Julia yelled out. "Your snake is attacking me again."

All of the students stared at Julia, and Mr. Johnston turned away from the blackboard and toward the commotion. The boa was wrapping itself around one of Julia's legs, pinning it up against one of the legs of her desk.

"Just ignore him," Mr. Johnston said.

"Ignore him?" Julia exclaimed. "He's got one of my legs!"

"Just take him off your leg," Mr. Johnston said.

"I don't know how!" Julia answered. She sounded desperate.

Mr. Johnston shook his head slowly and clucked like a chicken. Everybody started to laugh. "Can *somebody* please help Julia?"

Half a dozen kids raised their hands and screamed out requests to help.

"Ricky, can you do it, please?" he asked.

I smiled. I figured he was going to ask me. Most of the kids had gotten comfortable with Mr. Johnston's snake, but I was more than comfortable.

I got up from my seat and crossed to Julia's desk. I grabbed the boa by the tail. That's the best way to get a large constrictor to release its prey. Something about the way their muscles work. I started to unwind it from her leg. It didn't seem to want to let go and it wasn't easy to work it free from around her leg and the legs of the desk and chair.

"Please hurry," Julia pleaded.

Finally getting it loose, I lifted it up and placed it on my shoulders, around the back of my neck. It felt warm. People who don't know snakes always think that they're wet and slimy and cold. They *can* be cold— as cold as the air temperature—or really warm if it's hot out. This one was also very, very smooth. Bogart had recently shed his skin— snakes do that when they grow—and the new skin was unblemished, smooth and soft.

"Thanks," Julia said as I stood up.

Julia was pretty cool about the snake. She obviously didn't like it but she didn't act like some students who got all shivery just looking at it. There really wasn't much to be afraid of, because even a snake that size really couldn't do much harm to a big kid. Now, a cat or a small dog would be a different matter.

"I think you'd better put him back in his pen, Ricky," Mr. Johnston said. "Cell biology is pretty tricky stuff and I'd like everybody to focus up on the blackboard."

I started toward the back of the class. Bogart had a large case, an old bookshelf that was twice as long as him and taller than me. There was a water bowl, sand, and lots of tree branches placed at different levels for him to climb. Boas love to climb. In the jungle they usually catch their prey by dropping out of trees on top of them.

I uncoiled him from around my shoulders and placed him gently in the pen. I then took the glass that fronted the whole container and slid it closed. There, now he wouldn't be bothering anybody else today.

As Mr. Johnston continued to teach his lesson, I walked slowly back to my seat. I loved being here. This was my favourite place in the whole school. Actually, it was one of my favourite places in the whole world. Mr.

Johnston thought about animals the same way I did. His whole science room was just filled with them. He had even more animals than I had in my room. The walls of his class were lined with cages and pens and aquariums and terrariums. They were filled with fish and turtles and gerbils and rats and rabbits and lizards and snakes. They were part of his lessons, and we got to study them, hold them, play with them. And some of us . . . like me . . . got to be special helpers. It meant I had to do things like clean cages, and I had enough of that to do with my own animals, but it also meant being able to spend more time with the animals. That's how I spent at least half of my lunch hours.

I took my seat as Mr. Johnston continued to review the lessons we'd had on cell biology. I didn't really need a review. I looked over my shoulder at Bogart, who was settling into one of the branches at the top of the pen.

Of all the animals, Bogart was the most special. Mr. Johnston had had him for almost ten years. Mr. Johnston wasn't really very old, so that meant he couldn't have been much older than us when he first got the snake. He told us the story about having Bogart that first day and holding him up and looking him right in the eyes . . . and Bogart sinking his fangs into Mr. Johnston's nose! Boa constrictors don't have any poison, but they still bite to get a grip on their prey.

Bogart now spent the school year in Mr. Johnston's class, and each summer he went home and stayed in Mr. Johnston's house, in the basement. When Mr. Johnston went away, even for a couple of weeks, he just left Bogart down there by himself—safely locked in. One of the great things about snakes is that they don't need constant care. You feed them, leave some water, and they're okay for a long time. Bogart was just one of the cool things about Mr. Johnston. Actually, almost everything about Mr. Johnston was cool. He dressed in the same sort of clothes that we kids wore—I never saw him in a tie or suit. And when we came into class, he'd sometimes have music playing, the same music I listened to on the radio. And when kids talked, he knew the expressions we used. He was one cool teacher . . . with one cool wife. Mr. Johnston had gotten married over the summer and his new wife had dropped in one day to see him in September. She was beautiful . . . and she liked animals. That's what I wanted some day—to marry somebody who liked animals.

Suddenly the bell rang, signalling the end of class. People started to grab their books and talk and fidget in their seats.

"Class dismissed!" Mr. Johnston called out over the din. "But remember . . . test tomorrow!"

Some kids groaned, but I didn't care. A test was just a test, and I was pretty sure I wasn't going to get anything less than perfect on it. I gathered up my books, stuffed them in my backpack and started to leave.

"Ricky," Mr. Johnston said.

I turned around.

"Thanks for taking care of Bogart."

"No problem," I replied. "Do you need help at lunch?"

"A couple of kids have volunteered to clean out some of the pens, but I'm sure they could use a hand."

I nodded. "See you at lunch."

Augie was waiting in the hall just outside the door.

"Ugh . . . a test tomorrow."

I shrugged. "It's not hard stuff."

"Maybe not for you, but all this cell division and osmosis stuff is hard to remember."

"Not if you study," I suggested.

"Don't tell me you've studied already!"

"Just a bit on the weekend."

"Why would you do that? He didn't say anything about a test last week."

I shook my head. "There's always a test, Augie. Do you think these teachers talk just to hear their own voices?"

"Well . . ."

"It was just a question of *when* there was going to be a test. So I started studying early, that's all."

"That doesn't help me. It's too late for early. So . . ."

"I know, I know. Come on over to my place after school and we'll study. Okay?"

"Thanks," he said, patting me on the back. "I don't know what I'd do without you."

I smiled and thought the same thing about him.

Chapter Four

I worked hard to peel the last of the potatoes. Starch sprayed up into the air as I furiously dug in the peeler and the little scraps of skin flew off and into the sink. Finished, I put the potato under running water and washed off the dirt. I placed it on the cutting board and carefully cut it into eight pieces, and then swept them off and into the pot of water. That was the last of them. Now all I had to do was remember to put them on the stove so they could start to boil before my father got home. That was at least an hour and a half away. He worked at the other end of the city and he usually arrived home a little bit before five-thirty. Sometimes it was even later, if the traffic was bad along Highway 401. I hated when he was late . . . just hated it. The news was always filled with stories about traffic accidents. I'd read where car crashes were the most common way that people my father's age died. I didn't need anybody else to die— ever again.

I looked at the clock on the wall. Augie would be over in about fifteen minutes to study. That left me just

enough time to finish cleaning up the kitchen and—
There was a heavy knock on the door and Candy
scrambled down the hall, barking and snarling as she
ran. I figured Augie must be really worried about the
test to get here so early.

"Coming!" I yelled out.

I grabbed Candy by the collar and forcibly dragged
her away. She didn't want to come along and it was a
struggle.

"Hang on!" I called as I pulled her down the hall,
through the living room and towards the basement. I
pushed her onto the landing and closed the door, locking her away.

The knocking came again, louder and harder and
longer.

"Hold your horses!" I went to throw open the front
door. "We still have plenty of time to—" I stopped
myself. It wasn't Augie. It was a girl. A girl with long
blonde hair. An older girl. And she was holding a big
orange marmalade cat.

"Are you Ricky?" she asked.

"Um . . . yeah."

"You don't know me, but my name is Jessica. I heard
that you take care of animals."

Great, she wants to give me a cat. My father already
told me I couldn't have any more cats.

"Can you help my cat?" Jessica asked.

"Your cat?" I said blankly.

"His leg is hurt."

"Leg?"

"One of the back ones. It's hurt. Please, can you help fix my cat?"

I felt relieved. She didn't want to give it to me, she just wanted me to fix it up.

"Sure . . . I guess . . . maybe . . . what's wrong with its leg?"

"This," Jessica said as she turned her cat around. The back left foot was badly swollen.

"Wow, that doesn't look good. Here, let me have him," I said, taking the cat from her arms and starting back into the house.

"Wait!" she said. "Can I come along too?"

"Yeah, of course, sure," I replied, over my shoulder as I walked down the hall to the kitchen. I pulled out a chair, sat down and placed the cat on the table. I was glad I hadn't had time to set the table for dinner. The cat stood there, holding up its back foot so it barely touched the table, balancing on its other three legs.

"You're a nice kitty," I said as I rubbed my hand against the side of its head. The cat pressed against my hand in response.

"Can you hold him there for a second?" I asked.

She nodded and took hold of her cat.

I stood up and walked across the kitchen to the cupboard where we kept the food for the animals. I pulled out a box and removed a couple of cat treats—

little flavoured morsels that my cats loved. I kept one in my hand and tucked the rest away in the front right pocket of my jeans.

"Here you go, boy," I said as I held out my hand to the cat, offering the treat.

Carefully the cat took it from my hand.

"When did you first notice the problem?" I asked.

"The day before yesterday I thought there was something wrong—he was walking a little funny. And then yesterday he was limping even worse, and today he won't even walk on it."

"It looks infected."

I ran my hand along the cat's back and then slowly, carefully, down the leg toward the injury. I could feel the animal tense up as my hand got close. It must have really hurt.

"Can you do anything?" Jessica asked.

"It doesn't look good. Maybe you should take it to a vet."

She took a deep breath and sighed loudly. I looked away from the cat and up at her. She looked like she was about to cry.

"My father said he didn't want the cat in the first place . . . and he doesn't want to spend money for a vet. He said that he didn't care if the cat lived or . . ." She sniffled loudly. "Can't you fix it?" she pleaded.

"I can try. I'll be back in a minute."

I left the kitchen and hurried up to my room. I rummaged around in my closet, pushing things aside until I found what I was looking for: an old black sports bag. As I turned and started down the stairs again, there was another knock on the door. I could hear Candy howling from the basement. I ran to the door and threw it open. This time it was Augie.

"Come on in," I said as I turned away and started back to the kitchen. "We can start studying as soon as I take care of one thing."

"I need to start right away!" Augie protested as he followed me.

"It'll only take a few minutes. I have to take care of an animal that needs—"

"Can't your stupid animals wait until—" Augie suddenly stopped as he entered the kitchen and saw Jessica sitting at the table.

"It's my cat and he's not stupid!" Jessica said.

"I . . . I . . . I didn't mean anything . . . I just . . ." Augie stammered.

It was unusual to see him having trouble talking. I looked at Augie in surprise. I couldn't believe him not being able to talk to a girl. I didn't like to see him like that.

"This is my friend, Augie," I said. "And it's lucky that he came along. He knows all about animals."

"He does?" Jessica asked.

For a second Augie looked at me as though I'd lost my mind. Then he caught himself and nodded knowingly.

"I was thinking I should bathe the wound in Epsom salts and then give some antibiotics," I said. "Do you think that's the right thing to do?" I asked, turning to Augie.

He adopted a thoughtful look—I knew that didn't necessarily mean he was thinking about anything, but it looked impressive.

"Exactly what I would have recommended," he finally said.

"Good. Do you think you can get me the basin from the sink and fill it up with lukewarm water?" I asked.

"Sure, I'll—" Jessica started to say.

"No, not you. Augie, can you get it?"

He shrugged, nodded, and went to follow the directions.

I opened the zipper on the sports bag and started to remove things. First I took out a plastic bag filled with Epsom salts. I knew that a salt bath was good for almost all infections, including scratches and bites. I'd used a lot of it myself after being scratched or bitten by assorted animals. Next I pulled out a thick pair of canvas gardening gloves. I was going to try to avoid any new scratches or bites.

"Here's the water," Augie said as he plopped the

basin on the table, some water splashing over the sides.

I put my hand in it. It was about the right temperature. I would have liked it maybe a little warmer, but it really didn't matter. The cat wasn't going to be happy with it no matter what the temperature was.

Next I took the bag of Epsom salts and dumped in a few large lumps. With my hand I stirred it around so the salt would dissolve in the water. Satisfied, I dried my hands on my shirt and slipped on the gloves.

"What's your cat's name?" I asked.

"Garfield."

Now, that was original. "Well, Garfield isn't going to like this very much."

I picked up the cat carefully and then positioned him so that the infected foot would go into the basin. Garfield recoiled at the first touch of water and struggled to get away. I held on firmly with one hand, while I stroked him behind the ears with the other.

"It's okay, boy. He's just trying to help you," Jessica said softly.

"This will help to draw off the infection and disinfect the surface area so no new infection can develop," I said.

"And that'll be enough?" she asked.

"Not by itself. He'll also need some medicine to fight off the internal infection."

"But where will I get that?" Jessica asked.

"Go into my bag. There's a bottle of pills in there."

She peered inside the bag and fished around with her hands until she found the bottle.

"Do you mean these?"

"That's them," I said. "Open it up."

She undid the cap. "What is this?"

"Antibiotics."

"You have antibiotics for cats?" It sounded as though she had doubts.

"It's not for cats, but it'll work for cats. Can you hand me one of the small pieces in the bottle?" I asked.

She tipped the bottle and a couple of dozen little brown, broken pill pieces fell into her hand.

"Where did you get those from?" Augie asked.

"My doctor."

"You mean veterinarian?" Jessica asked.

"No, my doctor. It was given to me when I had an ear infection last year."

"You're giving my cat the same medication that you were taking?" Jessica asked in disbelief.

I shrugged. "Why not? We're both animals; I'm just a bigger animal. That's why I've broken them into pieces. I'm about ten times as big as the average cat and I've broken the pills into ten parts. Hand me one little piece."

Jessica looked down at the pieces in her hand but didn't move. She seemed concerned.

"Don't worry," I reassured her. "I've used them for my cats before."

She picked one up and handed it to me. I put it down on the table, removed one glove and picked up the piece in my bare hand.

"The secret is to get it into the very back of the mouth," I explained. I held the cat tightly by the head with one hand and pried open its mouth with my other hand. It struggled and strained and tried to dig in its back feet. I felt a sharp pain as claws dug into my skin above my gloved hand. I moved my hand to shake the claws free, but I still held the cat firmly. Garfield's mouth popped open, and I pushed two fingers in. Gingerly I deposited the pill on the very back of his tongue. He gagged and coughed as I removed my fingers, and then I proceeded to stroke his throat to massage the pill down.

"There, he swallowed it," I said.

"And Garfield will be all right now?" Jessica asked.

I nodded my head. "I'm no vet, but I think so. I'll give you eleven more pieces of the pills. You have to give him two more today and then three a day for the next three days."

"I have to do that?"

"Yep, as well as bathe the foot three times a day. I'll give you some of the Epsom salts."

"But . . . but . . . I don't think I can do it."

"It's not hard."

Jessica didn't look convinced.

I sighed. "Bring Garfield back here around eight tonight."

Her face brightened. "Thank you, thank you so much!" she exclaimed.

"And then tomorrow morning before school."

"What time tomorrow morning?" Jessica asked.

"It has to be early. I have to leave for school by eight-thirty."

"Or *earlier*," Augie said, giving me a dirty look.

"That won't work. I have cheerleading practice tomorrow before school."

"You're a cheerleader?" Augie said.

She nodded. She did look like a cheerleader.

"What school do you go to?" Augie asked.

"Oakwood," she answered.

That meant she was in high school, which made her at least two years older than me.

"Do you live far from here?"

"Not too far. I live on Silverthorn, just a few houses north of St. Clair."

"That's right by our school," I said. "We pass by your place every day on our way to and from school."

"Say . . . maybe I shouldn't ask . . ." Jessica said, "but do you think that you could drop by my place tomorrow morning on the way to school to do the treatment?" She smiled and her eyes twinkled.

I got the feeling that she was used to getting her way.

"I don't know if—"

"It would be *our* pleasure," Augie said, cutting me off abruptly.

"It would?" I said.

"Of course we wouldn't mind," he continued.

"We?"

"Yes, *we*," he said, giving me a look that told me to button it. "Somebody has to help you and *Jessica*."

The way he said *Jessica*, sort of soft and smooth and sweet, left no doubt in my mind whom he wanted to help . . . or to get to know better. I admired his persistence, although I thought he was wasting his time with Jessica. It wasn't just that she was older than us, in high school, but she was . . . well, a cheerleader, and pretty.

Augie was always joking that girls his age didn't fully appreciate him and he should only ask out "older women." That wasn't a problem for me because everybody was already older than me.

"I appreciate this so much!" Jessica gushed. "Thank you both!"

"No, no, it's our pleasure to offer our expertise to help an animal in need," Augie said.

"Give me your address when you bring the cat back tonight."

"Sure. You want me back around eight?" Jessica asked.

"Eight is good."

"Of course, I won't be around then," Augie said. "But I'll see you tomorrow morning."

"Um . . . remember, I have cheerleading practice. I'll probably be gone by the time you get there, but somebody will be home—my mother for sure."

Augie's face visibly deflated.

"It doesn't matter who's there, as long as Garfield's there," I said.

"Great. I'll see you tonight." Jessica rose and picked up Garfield.

I stood up as well and walked her to the door, while Augie remained seated at the table.

"And Jessica, you have to promise me something," I said.

"Sure, what?"

"I hope this'll work—you know, fix Garfield—but if it doesn't . . . if he isn't getting better in the next few days, you have to take him to the vet. Okay?"

"You mean this might not work? Garfield might not get better?" she asked anxiously.

"I'm just saying, just in case . . . okay?"

She nodded. "See you tonight."

I walked back to the kitchen. "Don't look so disappointed," I said.

"Why not? I *am* disappointed. She won't be there, so she can't succumb to my charms. And I was just starting to grow on her."

"You were?"

"Of course I was. Couldn't you tell?"

"I guess I was so busy taking care of the cat that I missed that part. But I still don't see why you're disappointed. You're always talking about 'older women,' right?"

"Yeah."

"So, remember who's definitely going to be there tomorrow."

"Who?"

"Her mother."

Chapter Five

"I don't even know why I'm going along," Augie said.

"Because you promised," I said.

"But she won't even be there, so she won't know if I broke my promise."

"I'm not talking about the promise you made to her. You promised *me*," I reminded him.

After Jessica left, Augie had tried to weasel out of coming with me. I told him that was fine with me—as long as he didn't need my help to study, I didn't need his help with the cat. We reached a deal.

Actually, I never had a single doubt that he'd come with me. Augie always kept his word—even when he didn't give it. He was probably the person I counted on the most in the whole world. I always did really well in school—it was the rest of life that confused me. Augie understood all that stuff that I didn't, and I relied on him.

"This isn't going to take long, is it?" Augie asked.

"No longer than it took yesterday after school. Of course, it'll go a lot faster if you help this time."

"I helped before!" Augie protested. "Who do you think filled the basin with water yesterday?"

"I meant, like, hold down the cat to bathe its foot or feed it the pill."

"So that it can rip open my arm too?" he asked, pointing at the gash on my arm.

Thank goodness Garfield had ripped only my arm and not my shirt. Arms repair themselves for free, but clothes have to be repaired or replaced. There was nobody at my house who could do the first, and we didn't have money for the second.

"It would certainly impress Jessica if you helped me more."

"Yeah, you're right . . ." Augie paused. "But she won't be there to see it."

"You never know, maybe she got thinking about seeing you this morning and decided to skip her cheerleading practice."

"Do you really think that she could be— "

I started to chuckle, and Augie realized I was putting him on.

"There it is," I said, pointing to a house. "Six Silverthorn Avenue."

We walked up the path, up the stairs, and crossed the porch. I pushed the doorbell and heard it ringing inside.

"Remember, in and out fast," Augie said.

"I'll move as fast as— "

The door swung wide and my mouth dropped open in shock. There was Elyse, a girl from our school—the most popular girl in our school, and the girl Augie had the biggest crush on. She had just started at Osler in September, and Augie had already spent a whole lot of time trying to impress her. So far, the only way he'd impressed her was the wrong way.

"I'm sorry . . ." I sputtered. "We must have the wrong place."

"Yeah, the wrong place," Augie echoed.

"We were just looking for a cat," I added.

"This isn't the wrong place," Elyse said. "You're here to take care of Garfield, aren't you?"

"Garfield is your cat?" I asked.

"Mine and my sister's."

"Jessica is your sister?" Augie asked.

"Yeah. I was expecting you," she said to me. "But not you," she added, aiming a finger at Augie.

"He's here to help."

"He can't do it without me," Augie told her.

"I thought you were the expert on animals?" Elyse said, looking at me.

"I *am* the expert, but I need Augie's help. He's going to hold the cat while we bathe its foot. We don't have that much time before school, so can we come in?"

"Sure, of course," she said as she pulled the door open further and ushered us into the house. "Garfield's in his basket in the kitchen."

We followed her down the hall and into the kitchen. A woman—I guessed it was her mother—was sitting at the table, eating a bowl of cereal.

"Good morning," she said. "I wasn't expecting two of you."

"One is the helper," Elyse said.

"I see, and which one of you is Ricky?"

"Um . . . I am," I stuttered, surprised she knew my name.

"Elyse told me all about you."

"She did?"

"Yes, she mentioned how knowledgeable you are about animals and how well you do in school and how you're going to be a vet when you grow up."

I felt myself start to blush.

"And your name is?" she asked, turning to Augie.

"I'm Augie."

"Augie? And do you go to school with Elyse?"

"We're in the same homeroom . . . all three of us."

"I just don't remember Elyse mentioning you, but there are so many new kids and new names that it's hard to keep track." She paused. "I must admit that I was a bit hesitant when Elyse suggested we bring Garfield to you, but she was right—he already seems to be getting better."

"Great, fantastic!" I blurted out. "Let me have a look at him."

Garfield was curled up in his basket in the corner of

the kitchen. Elyse gently picked him up and brought him over.

"Put him down on the table," I said.

"Cats aren't allowed on the kitchen table," Elyse's mother said.

"But I need a place, like an examination table, where I can work."

Elyse looked at her mother. "Mom?"

She shook her head slowly. "All right, but first we need to clear away the breakfast dishes so there's space."

"Let me help," I offered as I joined her in picking up dishes and plates and moving them to the counter.

"Thank you very much," she said. "So you're not only an animal expert, but you know how to help around the house."

"I'm used to doing things," I said.

"Then, your mother has trained you well," she said.

I didn't know what to say so I just kept moving dishes. It always felt strange when people talked about my mother ... what was I supposed to say? I don't have a mother. Or, we lost her. That made it sound like she wandered away. Or should I say the 'd' word? She died. We finished clearing away the last of the dishes.

"We'll need a basin with warm water to bathe the wound," Augie said.

I was so grateful he'd changed the subject for me.

Augie knew I didn't want to talk about my mother. Augie always knew stuff.

"I'll get that," Elyse's mother volunteered.

I took the cat from Elyse, took a seat, and placed him on the table. The foot still looked swollen, but it was encouraging that he was touching it down on the table, putting weight on it. I took a cat treat out of my pocket and offered it to Garfield. He took it from my fingers and swallowed it.

"Good cat," I said as I scratched behind his ear, and he pressed against my hand. He was a nice cat.

"How do you think it happened?" Elyse asked.

"Is he an outdoor cat?" I asked.

"Mostly he stays in the house, but he does go out sometimes."

"It could be a bite that he got in a fight—"

"He was bitten by another cat?" she exclaimed.

"Or maybe a dog, or a raccoon, or even a skunk."

"A skunk! You mean there are skunks around here?" Elyse asked.

"Lots of them, but come to think of it, I don't think it could have been a skunk, or your cat would have been sprayed, as well," I said, rethinking that option. "Or maybe his foot just got caught in something, or he stepped on a rusty nail. It's hard to tell."

"Here's the water," Elyse's mother said as she returned to the kitchen, carrying a yellow basin.

I could tell by Garfield's reaction that he remembered what had happened the last time a basin of water was placed beside him on a table. I prepared the water with the Epsom salts and gave the cat another treat, which he wolfed down.

"Good cat," I said again, continuing to stroke his back with my other hand. He rose on his toes, his back stretching upward to meet my hand.

"Okay, Augie, pick him up and put him back down so his infected foot is in the basin."

"Me?" he asked in alarm.

"Of course you . . . unless you'd rather give him his pill?"

His eyes grew wide. I knew he didn't want to do that. I also knew that he didn't want to hold the cat in the basin, but he really didn't have much choice, standing there with Elyse and her mother looking on.

Reluctantly and tentatively he picked up Garfield. He shifted the cat over and plopped him down so both back feet were in the basin. Garfield struggled to escape, his back feet scrambling, throwing water out of the basin, all over the table and up into Augie's face. Augie recoiled from the salty water, but tightened his grip, forcing Garfield to remain in place.

"Would you boys like something to drink?" Elyse's mother asked.

"I'm okay," I replied.

"A coffee would be nice," Augie answered. "Double, double, please."

She chuckled at his humour. "Why don't I get all three of you a glass of milk, and a few cookies to go along."

"Thanks," I replied as she went to the cupboard and got out some glasses.

"Are you two ready for the science test today?" Elyse offered.

"Definitely," I offered.

"No problem," Augie agreed.

"I wish I could be that confident," Elyse said. "I'm still not sure about some of it."

"What part?" I asked.

"Mainly about osmosis."

"That can be confusing," Augie agreed. "You just have to remember about the type of membrane and the concentration of solutions on either side of the membrane to determine if osmosis will take place."

"It sounds like you know what you're talking about," Elyse's mother said as she put down the glasses and started to pour the milk.

"I studied all last night," Elyse said. "And it didn't seem to help that much."

"We studied last night too," I said. "Augie came over to my place."

"You studied together?" Elyse's mother asked.

"We always do," Augie said. "It helps."

Helps Augie is what I thought, but of course I didn't say anything.

"If you'd like, you can study with us the next time," I said to Elyse, without really thinking about it.

"I could?" she said.

"She could?" Augie looked astonished by my invitation.

"You wouldn't mind, would you?" I asked him.

"No, of course not!"

"That's a very nice offer," Elyse's mother said.

"It's no problem," Augie said. "Has Garfield been in the water long enough?"

I nodded.

Augie picked up Garfield and placed him on a towel that Elyse had put down on the table beside the basin. The cat lifted one foot and then the other, shaking them, sending a fine mist into the air. I was very pleased to see him lift the one back leg—the one that wasn't infected—and place all his weight on the bad foot.

"All done. We'd better get going or we'll be late for school," I said.

"But what about the pill?" Elyse asked.

"Already done."

"It is?" Augie exclaimed.

I nodded my head as I pulled out another cat treat. "It was buried inside the second treat I gave to Garfield."

"Very smart," Elyse's mother commented.

I smiled. It was even smarter than she thought, since I'd basically tricked Augie into holding the cat because he didn't know the other job had already been done.

"If you'd like, we can explain osmosis to you on the way to school," I said.

"That would be great! Just let me get my things and I'll be right back down," Elyse said as she jumped up from the table.

Augie and I started to stand.

"Hold on, both of you!" Elyse's mother said. "Neither of you leaves until you drain those glasses of milk and eat at least two cookies each. Don't worry, you have plenty of time. Elyse always takes forever to get ready."

"Thanks," Augie said, and we both sat back down.

"Jessica was telling me all about the animals you have as pets," Elyse's mother said. "I couldn't believe it when she told me you had an alligator."

"It isn't that big."

"Big enough to take off a finger or two," Augie added.

"And she said you had squirrels and a groundhog—"

"*Two* groundhogs," I corrected.

"And lots of other pets. Where did they all come from?" she asked.

"A few of them, like the alligator, I bought, but most of them just sort of found me."

"Found you?"

"Sometimes they just show up at my door, either by themselves or 'cause somebody brings them to me. That's how I got the groundhogs and the grouse."

Elyse's mother must have noticed that I glanced anxiously at my watch because she volunteered to hurry her daughter along.

"I don't understand you," Augie said to me after she left the room.

"What do you mean?"

"You always say you can't talk to girls."

"I can't!" I protested.

"Sure, right. Didn't you just invite the prettiest girl in the school to come over to your house to study with us sometime?"

"Well . . ."

"Well, nothing. You done good. I just hope she hurries up. Walking her to school will be nice. Being late for school would be not so nice. And can you do me a favour?"

"Sure . . . maybe . . . it depends."

"Could you let me explain osmosis to her?"

"Yeah, that's no problem. But why?"

"She already knows you're smart. I'd like her to think I'm smart too."

Chapter Six

"So, did I do well explaining things to Elyse?" Augie asked as he worked his combination lock.

"Really well. You really understand this stuff. You're going to ace the test."

"I guess we'll see. Let's hurry."

I grabbed my books, the ones I'd need for science, history and then math, which we had just before lunch. I slammed the door closed, clicked the lock and then took two steps down the hall. I stopped, went back and checked to make sure it was locked.

"Hurry up!" Augie called from down the hall.

I hurried after him, going fast but not running. Running in the halls meant detentions.

I felt like a fish swimming upstream as I fought my way through the crowd, trying to catch up to Augie and get to class. There were always so many kids in the hall because there were so many kids in the school. It was a huge school with more than six hundred students. The strange thing, though, was that it seemed like Augie knew almost all of them—at least, everybody in grade eight—by name. And the few that he didn't know all seemed to know him.

"We'll just make it," Augie said as we turned off the main corridor, which held all the lockers, and into a stairwell. We took the steps two at a time and opened the door at the top leading to the second floor. Up ahead, I could see our whole class standing in front of Mr. Johnston's class. Why weren't they inside already?

Augie walked up to Elyse, who was standing with some of her friends.

"Why is everybody waiting out here?" he asked.

"The door's locked."

"That's strange," I said. "Mr. Johnston's always here early to take care of the animals, and I don't ever remember him being away."

"Mr. Johnston's away?" Augie asked.

"I didn't say that."

"If he is away, does that mean we won't have a test?" Augie asked hopefully.

"That only means we won't have a test *today*," I said. "But we will have a test, tomorrow or the next day or whenever."

"You mean I'll have to remember this stuff for a few more days? That's not possible," he said, shaking his head emphatically. "My head will explode, or at least start leaking out bits of information, you know, like in osmosis."

I couldn't help but smile. Sometimes his head did

seem like a semi-permeable membrane, so he was right—it could start dripping out!

"We need that test today!" Augie said, raising his voice. He pushed through the crowd toward the classroom door. I followed in his wake.

"What are you going to do?" I asked.

"Pound on the door. Somebody's got to be in there, like a supply teacher or somebody. I want my test! I demand my test!" Augie said loudly.

He raised his hand to knock on the door, then stopped. We both saw it at the same instant—the little glass window in the door was shattered. A piece of plywood had been nailed into place behind the few jagged pieces of glass that remained in the frame. Augie turned to me. His expression reflected my own confusion.

Just as I opened my mouth to say something, the PA came to life.

"Please stand for the playing of 'O Canada,'" called out the voice of our principal, Mr. MacDonald.

There was still some mumbling and shuffling, but kids quieted down.

"Please sing along," Augie said in a loud voice, doing a perfect imitation of our principal. "And remember, the first line of the song is, 'O Canada, our home and naked land.'"

Everybody broke up laughing.

"Very amusing," called out a deep voice. It was Mr.

Skully, our vice-principal. He had just stepped out of Mr. Johnston's room and was holding the door partially open.

"I wonder if our principal would be as impressed by your imitation as your classmates are?"

The first few notes of "O Canada" started to play and everybody froze in place. I kept my arms tightly against my side and sang along. The last notes of the song faded away.

"Augie, get in here, now," Mr. Skully said, holding the door slightly more open.

Poor Augie, he was going to get into trouble and—

"And Ricky, you come along, as well," Mr. Skully added.

"Me?" I asked in shock. I don't know what was more unexpected, that he wanted me to come too, or that he even knew my name. I did know which thought scared me more.

"But I wasn't doing anything!" I pleaded.

He scowled and hooked a finger at me. Numbly I stumbled forward, while the rest of the class stood, listening to the morning announcements. I squeezed through the opening of the door, careful not to make contact with Mr. Skully.

Why was he making me come? I hadn't done anything wrong and—

"My God, what happened?" I asked.

It looked like a tornado had passed through the

room. There were books and papers strewn everywhere. Some of the plants had been knocked over and dirt was all over the floor and— What about the animals? One of the big aquariums was smashed, and a couple of the cages were lying on their sides on the floor, and—wait—the entire front of Bogart's home, the sliding glass door, was shattered, lying in a million little pieces on the floor.

"Somebody, or more likely many people, broke into the school last night," Mr. Skully said.

"And they did this?" I asked in disbelief, my voice barely louder than a whisper.

"This and a whole lot of other things. They bashed a couple of the drinking fountains right off the walls, stole some AV equipment and did this to a number of the classrooms."

"That's awful," Augie said.

"Yes, it is," Mr. Skully agreed. "But you two can help."

"Do you want us to clean up?" I volunteered.

"Thank you for the offer, but that won't be necessary. The caretaking staff will be in shortly to start that job."

"But what can we do, then?" I asked.

"As you can see, some of the cages have been disturbed and some of the animals have gotten out. Mice and rats and gerbils . . . frogs . . . and I think some of the turtles and—"

"What about Bogart?" I asked. I don't see him!"

"He's . . . he's not here," Mr. Skully said. "He's with Mr. Johnston."

"So he's okay?" I asked.

Mr. Skully didn't answer, but he looked uneasy.

"Is Bogart all right?" I repeated.

"Mr. Johnston is looking after him—I'm sure he'll be fine. Why don't you boys stay here and work?" Mr. Skully said. "I can't leave the rest of your class in the hall unsupervised and I can't bring them in here. I'll find someplace for them to go."

He walked to the door and then stopped and turned around. "And, boys, please be careful, I don't want you to get cut or injured with all the broken glass and over-turned equipment."

He opened the door to leave, and the noise from our class, milling around in the hall outside the door, flooded in.

"Everybody settle down!" Mr. Skully yelled. The noise dropped off and then was sealed away when the door closed behind him.

Augie and I were alone in the room. The only noise was the squeaking of an exercise wheel in one of the cages. The cage was lying on the floor, upside down, with the little metal door on the side open. Augie walked over, picked up the cage and set it down on the counter, making sure the door was properly shut.

"At least this guy is okay," he said. "Although his

water bottle got smashed. Are there any replacement bottles around here?"

Yeah . . . maybe . . . I wasn't sure—everything was just so broken up.

"Ricky?"

"Yeah?"

"Are you okay?"

"I . . . I . . ." I shook my head. "I just don't know . . . where do we even begin?"

"With *this* hamster," Augie said. "You can't look at the whole room. Just focus on one little piece at a time. And that piece is this hamster, and he needs a drink. Understand?"

I nodded my head.

"Are there any other water bottles to replace this broken one?" he asked again.

I nodded again.

"Good. And do you know where they are?"

For the third time I nodded.

"Then . . . get one."

"Sure, okay," I mumbled, stumbling toward the back of the class where they were kept. I stepped on broken glass, which crunched under my feet, and around the other debris strewn on the floor.

I opened the cupboard. It was filled with bottles and beakers and test tubes. It was undisturbed—maybe the only place in the whole room that was. I reached in, grabbed a water bottle and filled it from the tap. I walked back, stepping around as much garbage as possible, and clipped it onto the cage. The hamster, smelling the water, rushed over and started drinking thirstily.

"Do you know how many animals and what kind of animals were in each cage?" Augie asked.

"More or less."

"That's what I thought. Take these." He handed me a pad of paper and a pen.

"I'm going to put the cages back onto the counters and shelves. You're going to follow behind me and rip off one piece of paper per cage. On that piece of paper you're going to list how many animals, and what type of animal is supposed to be there. Then put that piece of paper on the top of the cage. Understand?"

"Yeah."

"Then you'll search the cage. You'll look in the shavings or whatever is inside the cage because maybe more than just that one hamster stayed in the cage. Does that all make sense?"

"Perfect sense—that's a great plan!"

"Don't sound so surprised."

"I wasn't. Not at all. You always have good plans," I admitted. "It's just that I never understand . . ." I let the sentence trail off. This wasn't the time to be asking that question.

"Never understand what?" Augie asked.

"Nothing."

"Had to be something," Augie insisted as he turned to face me.

I swallowed hard. "Well . . ."

"Well, what?"

"It's just that . . . you're always thinking things through . . . planning—smart plans, really smart plans—and you understand people so well, but . . ."

"But why don't I do better in school. Right?"

I nodded.

"I wish I knew," Augie said with a sigh. "I wish I knew." He paused. He turned away and picked up another cage, placing it on the counter.

I made a note and put it on the first cage. There was one hamster still inside—five missing.

"There's no point in recapturing 'em if we can't keep them in the cages," Augie said. He picked up a cage that was bent out of shape as if someone had stepped on it. He used his considerable strength to reshape it into something that would hold the rats that made it their home.

I caught sight of movement in the cage, opened the little door on the top and reached in. There, nestled amongst the shavings, was a mother rat, with five little pink naked bodies nuzzled up to her belly nursing.

"Wow, I've never seen rats that little before," Augie said, peering in over my shoulder.

59

"They can't be more than a few hours old," I commented.

Unbelievable. Despite all of this, I couldn't help but smile.

The bell rang to signal the end of first period. Augie and I had done a lot in less than forty minutes. The cages were all back in place and a surprisingly large number of the animals had stayed in their cages, despite open doors and bent frames. We'd also already recaptured a number of the animals that had escaped, and had put them back in their pens. Some others had been found— but they were dead. There was nothing we could do about it.

On the floor right beneath the three smashed aquariums were dozens and dozens of dried-out carcasses of fish that had been so alive just yesterday. No longer brilliant red or blue or green or orange, they were now grey and brown and black. It was sad, but somehow right, that death had robbed the tropical fish of their vivid colours. I'd grabbed a broom and just swept them up. I wanted to get them out of sight before Mr. Johnston got back. He loved those fish. He loved all his animals so much.

Then I saw something that made my stomach flip. On the floor, in the corner, spread out with its legs and head extended, was one of the turtles. It was squashed flat, like a bug. How could this have . . . I couldn't stop myself from picturing the little turtle crawling away after its world was turned over and destroyed . . . slowly moving off along the floor, trying to get away . . . when a foot, a big ugly foot, smashed down on it. I shuddered. How could anybody do such a thing? But maybe it hadn't been done on purpose. Maybe it had been done by someone like me, walking across the room, tripping on things. Maybe it had been an accident.

And then I saw a second splattering, and a third and a fourth. Flattened turtles. This was no accident. Somebody had deliberately stomped on each one.

I felt my tongue grow thick and my chin start to quiver. I tried to sniff back the tears. I didn't want Augie to see me crying over a bunch of turtles. What would he think?

I heard the door open and turned around to look. It was Mr. Johnston. He looked awful—as sad and upset as I felt. I wished he hadn't come for a little while longer. We needed more time to clean up this mess.

"We've got a lot of them," I said, trying somehow to offer him a glimmer of hope.

He nodded. "Thank you, thank you, both," he said, his voice cracking over the last few words. "I knew I could count on you two."

"We'll keep working here," I said. "We'll take care of everything. How's Bogart doing?"

Mr. Johnston looked away. That was stupid. I shouldn't have asked. I shouldn't have said anything.

Mr. Johnston opened his mouth like he was going to say something, and then stopped himself. He sighed loudly and his whole body seemed to shudder. "Bogart is dead."

Chapter Seven

"He's dead. The people who broke in . . . they killed him . . . ?" I stammered.

"No," Mr. Johnston whispered.

"But . . . but you said he was dead."

"He is," Mr. Johnston said softly.

"But if they didn't kill him . . ."

"I did."

"You killed Bogart?" I couldn't believe my ears!

"He was hurt, badly hurt." It looked like he was having trouble speaking. "I think they must have stomped on him. A lot of his ribs were broken, and his eyes were . . . punched out."

I took a deep breath and tried to say something . . . but what?

"What do you mean, punched out?" Augie asked.

"It looked like they took something, maybe a compass from a math set, or a pencil, or a screw driver or . . . I don't know what, and they poked his eyes."

A shudder went up my spine and I felt ill.

"I can't even imagine," he said, shaking his head slowly.

"'That's awful," I said. "Poor Bogart, he would have been in so much pain."

"'That's why I had to do it," Mr. Johnston said. "I had to. I had to . . . put him out of his misery," he said, the words forcing themselves out. "I gave him an injection so he would just go to sleep."

I thought he was going to start crying. I knew how he felt, because that was exactly how I felt. I also knew that he was trying to fight back the tears as hard as I was.

"Poor old Bogart," Mr. Johnston said. "Never hurt anybody." He paused. "I can't even imagine somebody . . . somebody doing that."

Then I saw the first tears start to flow from his eyes. Even though I'd seen it coming, I was shocked. I'd never seen a teacher cry, never seen a man cry. I guess my father must have cried when my mother died, but I never saw him. Somehow, seeing Mr. Johnston in tears dried up the ones that were struggling to form in my eyes. He sniffled loudly and then wiped his eyes with the back of his hand.

"I need some time alone," Mr. Johnston said as he turned away from us and started to walk to the door.

I guess he didn't want us to see him cry.

"And boys—" He stood holding the door open with one hand, his back to us. "Thank you for everything you're doing to help. Thank you . . . so much," he said, his voice cracking over the final few words. And then he was gone.

Augie and I looked at each other. I struggled to find something to say, tried to put into words what I was feeling, but nothing came to my mind.

"We better keep working," Augie said.

I nodded. Augie was right. There was still a lot to do here, and there was nothing I could do to bring back Bogart or help Mr. Johnston. There was absolutely nothing I could do to make things better. . . except help clean up.

I struggled to take off my T-shirt. It was plastered to my body, soaked in sweat from the basketball tryout.

"That was a workout!" Augie said as he sat down beside me on the bench.

All around us the other kids trying out for the team—the senior team—were standing, or sitting, talking, laughing, and getting changed, either to leave for home or to take a shower before going. There was no way I was going to take a shower here. Something about standing around, naked, with a bunch of other naked guys while cold water came squirting out of the walls held no appeal for me at all. The times I *had* to do it—after gym class, or before we could go into the pool—was bad enough. When I had a choice, like after practice, I just changed and went home and had a bath. A bubble bath.

It was one of those secrets that I think everybody has. Sitting in a hot bath, the bubbles rising over the top of the tub, the door closed, a book in my hand and a can of Coke sitting on the ledge beside me was almost perfect. Nobody in the world, except for my father and my sister, knew that I took bubble baths. And there was no way I wanted anybody else ever to know.

"You did pretty good," I said as I took my towel and tried to wipe off some of the sweat.

"That's more than I can say about you," Augie said.

"I've done better."

"That's an understatement. You didn't take a single shot during the whole scrimmage."

"Shooting isn't everything," I said.

"Not everything, but you didn't do *anything*," he continued. "I couldn't believe a couple of those passes you tried to make."

He was right, of course. "I guess I just wasn't into it today."

"Look, if you just want to be on the junior team, don't even bother wasting your time coming to the senior tryouts."

"It isn't that," I said.

"Then, what?"

"I just couldn't stop thinking about the break-in."

"You and everybody else. That's all people talked about today," Augie said.

"I was trying to think what we could do about it."

"We cleaned up the room and found all those animals."

"I want to do more."

"Other than tracking down the people who did it, I can't figure out what more we can do."

"I thought about that too," I admitted, pulling on my pants over my shorts.

Augie gave me a horrified look. "You're not serious, are you? I heard the police found some stuff the guys who broke in must have dropped—some of it in the schoolyard and more out in the alley. They probably took off through that hole in the fence. It wouldn't surprise me if it was those high school guys. You know, Jimmie Saunders and his crew. You don't want to tangle with them . . . they'd *kill* you."

Of course Augie was right—it could have been Jimmie. He was one of the guys who had been roughing up kids for their lunch money. He was only a couple of years older than me, but he was more like a grown-up . . . a scary grown-up. Maybe they'd decided to move up to doing break-and-enters at the school. I figured if a person didn't have any respect for people, he probably wouldn't think twice about killing a snake.

"I could see people like Jimmie Saunders doing something like this," Augie said. "But that doesn't mean you're going to try to do something about it . . . right?"

"That's up to the police. Besides, that wouldn't help Mr. Johnston."

"So, what do you have in mind?" Augie asked.

"That's the problem. I don't have any idea whatso-ever," I admitted. "That's what I was thinking about all through school today."

"And on the court, as well."

"And on the court, as well. I better get going," I said, standing and doing up the last buttons on my shirt.

"What's the rush?"

"I've got to get home. I've got things to do," I explained. What I had to do was get supper started, but I didn't like to announce that to people.

"There's still plenty of time before your father gets home."

"There is, but remember I have to stop in and give Garfield another treatment on the way home."

"That's right!" Augie said, jumping to his feet. "And Elyse—I mean, Garfield needs our help too. Just give me a minute to get ready. I'll grab a quick shower and—"

"I don't have time for that."

Augie lifted up an arm and sniffed one of his armpits. "I stink. I don't want to go there when I stink. Couldn't I just wash up a little first?"

"No time. Either come now, or don't come."

"Fine," Augie said. "I'll come, but I'm not happy. If Elyse wrinkles her nose like she smells something bad, I'm going to point at you."

I still had to wait another ten minutes for Augie to get ready. He insisted on splashing on some aftershave, rolling on some deodorant and running a comb through his hair to try to flatten it out. Augie's hair was permanently frizzy.

"So, do you think she likes me?" Augie asked, as we walked up the street to Elyse's house.

"Does who like you?"

"Elyse, of course."

I shrugged. "Beats me—but why *wouldn't* she like you? You helped with her cat, and you explained things so she could understand osmosis better."

"Yeah, you're right! Why shouldn't she like me?" Augie exclaimed. We walked up the front path to her house.

"Because you stink?" I said with a smirk as I pushed the doorbell.

"Do I really?" Augie started to say when the front door opened and Elyse appeared.

"Hi, guys, come on in," she said. "I was beginning to think you'd forgotten."

"Of course we wouldn't forget," Augie said. "We had basketball."

"Are you two on the school team?" she asked.

"We're trying out," I said.

"Just a formality. We're two of the best players in the whole school," Augie added.

"And two of the most modest, as well," Elyse said.

I couldn't help but laugh as Augie cringed slightly.

"Could we see Garfield?" I asked. "I really have to get going soon."

"Sure, of course," she said.

We followed her into the kitchen. Garfield was sitting in his basket in the corner of the room.

"Bring him over here. Augie, can you fill the basin, please," I said, motioning to the container on the counter.

Elyse picked up her cat, while Augie went to the sink and started filling the basin with warm water and Epsom salts. She placed Garfield on the table in front of me.

"How's it going, boy?" I asked, rubbing him behind one of his ears. I reached into my pocket and pulled out a cat treat with a piece of pill lodged in it. Garfield readily took it from my hand and swallowed it. He rubbed against my hand. He didn't seem to be favouring the bad leg at all. I picked up Garfield and put his foot in the water. He didn't struggle nearly as hard this time.

"He seems a lot better," I noted.

"He is. And I want to thank you two so much," Elyse said.

"That's okay."

"I was thinking about Mr. Johnston, and how sad he must be about losing some of his animals," Elyse said.

"He was pretty upset," Augie said.

"I know how that is. I lost a cat."

"You did? When?"

"His name was Tigger—you know, like from Winnie-the-Pooh. He just disappeared. We searched for days and days."

"That's hard," I said. I'd lost two cats that way.

"And then, about two weeks after Tigger disappeared, my mother brought home Garfield. We still missed Tigger, but somehow having Garfield made it hurt less."

"Yeah, I guess that would help you to—" I stopped mid-sentence. That was it! "That's what we're going to do!" I shouted as I jumped up, releasing my grip on Garfield. He scurried away, spraying water as he leaped off the table.

"What are you talking about?" Augie demanded.

"I know what we have to do," I said, looking first at Augie and then at Elyse. "We have to buy Mr. Johnston another boa constrictor."

Chapter Eight

"You're joking, right?" Augie asked.

"No, I'm serious," I said, "we have to buy him another snake."

"But wouldn't that be expensive?"

"A boa as big as Bogart would probably cost one or two thousand dollars."

"Wow, you could buy a car with that much money," Augie pointed out.

"But we don't have to buy him one that big. We could get him a younger one, a smaller one—say, three feet long."

"And how much would that cost?"

"Not nearly as much. About four hundred dollars."

"That's still an awful lot. Do you have four hundred dollars?" Augie asked.

"Of course not, but I wasn't thinking that I'd pay for it all myself," I said.

"Hold on a second," Augie said, his hands in the air. "I like Mr. Johnston, but I don't have two hundred dollars to spend on a snake."

"Neither do I. I didn't mean just you and me could buy the snake," I explained. "I mean everybody could pitch in—everybody in the whole school. There are a few more than six hundred kids in the school, so all we need is for two out of three kids to give a dollar."

"And you think that all those kids are just going to walk up to you and hand you a buck?" Augie asked.

"Of course not. First off, they have to know to give the dollar."

"What are you going to do, go on the PA and ask everybody to come to our class and give you a dollar?"

"It's a little more complicated than that," I said.

"Of course it is!" Augie insisted.

"For one thing, we can't use the PA or it wouldn't be a surprise. I don't want Mr. Johnston to know anything about it."

"Why not?"

"A surprise is better." I turned to Elyse. "Like when you got Garfield. Didn't that make it even better that your mother surprised you?"

She nodded. "Yeah, it did. It made it even more specialer."

"Besides, if Mr. Johnston knew what was being organized, he'd probably try to stop it. You know what he's like—he wouldn't want anybody to go to all that trouble," I said.

"You're right," Augie agreed. "Especially the whole-lot-of-trouble part. Do you have any idea how long it would take for you to explain this to every kid in the school?"

"About twice as long as it would take for *two* people to explain it," I said.

"Two . . . as in you and *me*?" Augie asked.

"It's just that nobody knows everybody in the school the way you do, and it'll involve handling a lot of money, and you're good with money, and we'll have to organize it all and—"

"Yeah, yeah, yeah, but even with two people it will still take forever," Augie objected.

"What about if there were three people?" Elyse asked.

I smiled. "Are you volunteering to help?"

"It's the least I can do after you two took care of my cat. And I like Mr. Johnston, and I know how it feels to lose something that you love," she explained.

I looked at Augie. Elyse offering to help meant that Augie was in for sure.

"Well?" I asked Augie.

He nodded slowly. "Count me in."

"Great! Fantastic!" I exclaimed.

"Yeah, right, great," he mumbled. "So what's the plan?"

"I don't exactly have all the details thought out yet."

"Tell me what you have so far," Augie asked.

I shrugged. "I sort of told you what I have so far— we'll buy Mr. Johnston a new snake after collecting money from kids."

"That's it?"

"So far," I admitted. "I was hoping you'd be able to help me figure out the rest."

"You could help do that, couldn't you?" Elyse asked.

Augie sighed deeply. "Yes, I can do that too."

I shifted around restlessly and tried to untangle my feet from the bottom of my sleeping bag. No matter what I did I just couldn't seem to get to sleep. I plumped up my pillow, then doubled it over and pushed it back under my head. I guess it really wasn't what was *under* my head that was keeping me awake so much as what was *in* my head. Every time I closed my eyes I saw the science room all smashed up. The broken aquariums, the twisted cages, the little flattened turtles, the brown corpses of the fish drying up on the floor. And then I thought about Mr. Johnston's having to put Bogart to sleep. What sort of people would have done all of that? No, they weren't even people . . .what sort of *monsters* could cause all that damage and pain?

And then I thought about what Augie and Elyse and I were going to try to do. Augie and I had agreed we'd meet before school tomorrow. I had a few ideas, but there was still a lot I hadn't been able to think through. It was going to be, like Augie had tried to warn me, a really hard thing to do. But we could figure it out. I was one-hundred-percent certain of that . . . well, almost one-hundred-percent certain.

I ran the toes of my left foot along the inside part of the zipper of the sleeping bag. The metal felt cold. It was something I'd been doing—a habit—when I was trying to get to sleep; at least for the past few months. Before that, I used to have sheets on my bed. But one wash day they hadn't been dry when it was time to make my bed and go to sleep, so I unrolled my sleeping bag and used that. And ever since then, I'd used my sleeping bag. It just seemed easier than making the bed every morning, and it saved my father from having to wash out my sheets every couple of weeks. It was better for everybody.

And then, just as I was starting to drift off, I thought about Mr. Johnston again, and something Elyse had said—about how she knew what it was like to lose something you loved. And I couldn't help thinking about the things I'd lost, and how afraid I was of losing anything more— Wait a second, I hadn't said my prayers!

I climbed out of my sleeping bag and dropped to my knees. I took a look over my shoulder to see if anybody was watching me. My sister Janice was in her room and my father was downstairs working. I didn't like anybody to see me saying my prayers. Janice said it was stupid. It's funny, because my sister and I used to be pretty close—she was just seven years older than me—but lately she'd been treating me like some dumb kid who didn't have a clue and whose only purpose in life was to bug her as much as possible. Of course I *was* pretty good at bugging her.

My father didn't think praying was stupid—just pointless. He said he stopped believing in God when my mother died. Strange, that was about the time I figured that I really started to need to believe in God even more.

"Dear God," I mumbled softly into my hands. "I had a good day today . . . thanks for that . . . and I hope things will work out good tomorrow too. I really don't want to trouble you about things—you have enough to take care of—but I hope things can work out with this snake. But if they don't, you know, I'll understand . . . 'cause things happen that I don't want and I know it's for a reason . . . right? So good night, thank you, I love you, and amen."

I got up off my knees, climbed back into my sleeping bag and snuggled into the material to get all warm. I shifted around anxiously.

I was glad I'd said my prayers—I really couldn't sleep

at night until I did—but I probably shouldn't have bothered asking God for anything. It wasn't just that He was
busy. It was just better not to pray for anything in partic-
ular. That way, at least you couldn't be disappointed.

Chapter Nine

"Are you sure about this?" I asked Augie. We'd finished lunch and were headed for the office.

"As sure as I was when we thought of it," he said. "We agreed on this plan, so we just have to follow it."

"But I was just thinking that maybe we could—"

"Could nothing. We need to talk to the office about what we want to do," he said, cutting me off. "We can't just start collecting money from all the kids without talking to the office. We could get in serious trouble."

"I guess you're right," I admitted.

"I know I'm right. Just let me do most of the talking."

"You can do *all* of the talking, as far as I'm concerned."

"It sounds like you're afraid of Mr. Skully," Augie said.

"Of course I'm afraid of Mr. Skully," I enthusiastically agreed. "Isn't everybody?"

"I used to be . . . you know, the first couple of dozen times I was sent down to the office. But after that he didn't seem so bad."

"I guess I just haven't had your experience," I said.

"I knew all those trips to the office would come in handy someday. Come on," Augie said as he held open the door to the office.

There were half a dozen kids sitting in chairs against the wall and another three or four standing at the counter. Two secretaries were behind the counter, one talking on the phone and the other talking to one of the kids. We waited our turn.

"What can I do for you, Augie?" the secretary asked.

I was impressed that she knew his name—but then, he was here a lot.

"We're here to see Mr. Skully," Augie answered, motioning to me.

"And who sent you down?" she asked.

"Nobody."

"Nobody sent you down? Did Mr. Skully ask you to come down?" She sounded suspicious.

"No, we just came on our own. We wanted to see him," Augie explained.

"And you didn't do anything wrong?" she asked.

"Nothing. We didn't do nothing wrong. We were just hoping he was free to talk to us."

"He is busy right now. He's in with a student and he does have a number of other students he has to see," she said, pointing to the boys waiting against the wall.

"Um, maybe we can come back later," I stammered, glad to have an excuse to leave.

"No, no, that's quite all right. I think you should

wait. It's not that often that students come down to the office who *want* to talk to the vice-principal. I'll see if he can squeeze you two in," she said.

At that moment Mr. Skully's closed door popped open and a kid, followed by Mr. Skully, walked out. The kid didn't look very happy. Actually, Mr. Skully didn't look too thrilled either. As the student walked away, the secretary went up to Mr. Skully. She said something to him—something I couldn't hear—and then she pointed to me and Augie. He scowled in our direction, motioned for us to come and then disappeared back into his office.

"Come on," Augie said.

I reluctantly followed him through a little swinging door that let us go behind the counter. We walked past the secretaries' desks and stopped at the open door. Mr. Skully was seated inside, his head down, studying the papers scattered across his desk.

"Yes, boys?" he said without looking up.

"Can we talk to you for a minute?" Augie asked.

I noticed Augie's voice didn't sound any more confident than I felt.

"A minute is about all that I have. Please sit down."

We sat in two of the seats opposite his desk.

"Now, what exactly is your problem?" he asked.

"We don't have a problem," Augie said.

"Then, why are you here?"

"We wanted to talk about the break-in and—"

"You have information about the break-in?" Mr. Skully said, suddenly looking up.

"No, no, we don't have information about it," Augie said. "But we heard that the police were over at the high school talking to some kids. Maybe even former Osler students. I mean, that would make sense, wouldn't it? They'd know where everything was."

I knew Augie was thinking about Jimmie and the other kids in the alley. We both certainly had our suspicions, but even mentioning Jimmie Saunders might get somebody beaten up.

"Obviously, boys, I'm not at liberty to discuss the police investigation with any students. When they know something definite, though, you can be sure it will become known. Is this what you wanted to see me about?"

"Actually," Augie began, "we wanted to ask you for a favour."

"What kind of a favour?" he asked, sounding as skeptical as his secretary had when we told her we weren't in any trouble.

"It's about Mr. Johnston and his boa constrictor," Augie said.

"What a tragedy," Mr. Skully said, shaking his head.

"Yes, sir," Augie said. "And we want to do something about it."

"You already did," he said. "I appreciate all the work

you did cleaning up the science room and recapturing the animals."

"Thank you, sir," Augie answered.

I'd never heard him call anybody "sir" before, and now he'd used that word twice in a row. Either he respected Mr. Skully, or he feared him.

"But we want to do more," Augie continued.

"I'm afraid there isn't much more that any of us can do," Mr. Skully said.

"But there is," I said, surprising myself by jumping in.

"There is?" Mr. Skully said, turning to me. "You're . . . um . . ."

"Ricky."

"Yes, of course. I just lost your name for a split second. It's hard to remember everybody when there are so many students in the school, but I know you. Weren't you on the basketball team last year?"

"Yeah . . . sir," I said, following Augie's example. "And I'm trying out again this year."

"Good for you!" he said. "And I know I see you around the school. You're almost always with Augie, aren't you?"

"Yes, sir."

"Strange," Mr. Skully said, a perplexed look on his face. "You two spend most of your time together, but I only ever see one of you down here at the office."

"That is strange," Augie said, nodding. "I've been trying to figure that one out myself."

Mr. Skully chuckled and a smile creased his face. "So what exactly do you two have in mind?"

"Tell him," Augie said, looking at me.

I took a deep breath. "We want to buy Mr. Johnston a new snake."

"A new boa constrictor?"

"Yeah . . . sir," I answered.

"That's a very kind thought, boys, but do you have any idea what it would cost to buy another snake as big as—"

"Close to a thousand dollars," I said, cutting in. "But we weren't going to buy one that big."

"Well, I'm sure that even a smaller one would still cost—"

"Just under four hundred dollars," I said, finishing his thought.

"Even if you could raise the money, I'm sure you can't just run down to the corner store and buy a boa constrictor," Mr. Skully said.

"No, but you can get one at Reptile World, and I'm sure four hundred dollars will cover it," I explained.

"Which brings us back to the original question of money."

"Yes, sir," Augie said. "And that's why we've come to speak to you."

"You want the school to give you the money?" he asked in disbelief.

"Not the school," I said. "Everybody *in* the school."

"Everybody?"

"Yeah. Everybody in the whole school. All the kids, and the teachers, too, if they want to contribute. We want to collect money from everybody."

"Is it all right if we do it?" Augie asked.

"Have you asked Mr. Johnston about any of this?" Mr. Skully asked.

"No, and we can't," I said.

"Why not?"

"We want it to be a surprise," Augie explained.

Mr. Skully laughed. "A surprise!"

"Yeah, we don't want him to know anything about it until we hand it to him. Wouldn't that be something?" I asked.

"It would be something, but it might also be impossible. There are hardly any secrets in a school. Just how do you propose to do this?"

"We want to talk to everybody in the school," Augie said. "Go to every single class and talk to the students."

"And when would you do that?"

"Today and tomorrow," Augie said. "We can do it all in two days."

"Do you think you can afford to miss two full days' worth of classes?" Mr. Skully asked.

"I'll help him make up the lost lessons," I offered.

"And who'll help *you* make it up?" Mr. Skully asked.

"Um . . . nobody."

"He doesn't need anybody," Augie said. "He's really smart."

"Is he?" Mr. Skully asked doubtfully. "I'll have to check with your homeroom teacher and—"

"Why don't you just check in the hall," Augie said.

Mr. Skully gave him a stern, questioning look.

"On the honour roll list on the wall. You gave Ricky the award for highest marks in grade seven last year. Remember?" Augie asked.

"Actually . . . come to think of it, I do remember."

"So, can we do it?" Augie asked.

Mr. Skully got up from his seat, walked over to the window and stared outside. I looked over at Augie and he gave me an "I don't know" look. We waited silently until finally, he turned back around.

"Do you know what a major part of my job involves, boys?"

"Um . . . not really," Augie said. "I guess it has a lot to do with yelling at people when they get in trouble."

"It's not quite that simple. Mostly what I deal with is problems. Problems with buses, or schedules, or students getting in trouble, or disputes between teachers and parents, or having repairmen fix whatever part of this school is breaking down. I deal with problems, that's my job. And the last thing in the world I need is another problem to deal with."

And we were giving him one more problem, a big problem, to deal with, I thought. Augie had been wrong, we never should have come to see him. We should have done it by ourselves and hoped the office didn't find out.

"But what you two are suggesting isn't a problem," he continued.

"It isn't?" I asked in disbelief.

"No, it isn't." He walked over until he was standing right over top of us. "It will be my pleasure to help you two in any way I can," Mr. Skully said. "In any way I can."

Chapter Ten

"Ladies and gentlemen," Mr. Yeoman began, and the whole class went quiet. "I want you to put down your pens for a few minutes and listen to a very important announcement by these two young men."

Mr. Yeoman sat down. Augie and I walked to the front of the room, and I knew every eye in the place was on us. It was a grade seven class, which should have made it less stressful than talking to a grade eight class, but it didn't. It was strange, but after having been with older kids the past few years, it made me nervous to be around kids my own age. Looking around the room I even noticed a couple of kids I knew—kids who I'd left behind in grade three when I got kicked up to grade five.

"My name is Augie and this is Ricky. We're grade eights, and we want to talk to you about something important," he began. "We know you haven't been in the school very long, so you probably don't know Mr. Johnston very well, but how many of you like him?"

Everybody's hand went up. That was a good way to start, but hardly a surprise. Mr. Johnston wasn't just one of the best teachers in the school, he was also the best-liked teacher in the school.

"And I guess you all know what happened to his snake during the break-in."

"That was awful," a girl in the front row said loudly.

"Yes, it was. How many of you would like to do something about that?"

Again everybody's hand shot up into the air.

"Even better. Here's our plan."

As Augie started to explain things, I started thinking about him. We'd been friends since the first day of grade five. We met on the first day. I don't remember a lot about that day, except that I was scared.

We all had to stand in line outside the grade five class. And I didn't know anybody. All I knew was that they were older than me, and most of them, even the girls, seemed to be bigger. Just down the hall, close enough that I could see them, were the rest of the kids from my grade three class. The kids I'd known and played with, and gone to school with since kinder-garten. My friends. They were standing together, laughing and talking, waiting to go into the grade four room, and I wished I could have been waiting outside that door. I knew that it was supposed to be some kind of honour to skip a grade, and it made my father really happy. But I wanted to be standing with them instead of staring at them from down the hall.

I was just kind of keeping my head down, trying not

to stick out, even though I knew I did, and this kid came up and started talking to me. He said hello and made a couple of jokes and told me his name was Augie. I thought it was a strange name, but I didn't care what he was called. It felt a lot better talking to somebody instead of standing there feeling stupid and alone. And Augie acted the opposite of how I felt. He was cool and confident and seemed to have everything together. And while I didn't say much to him, I could tell that he was friendly and nice . . . and he was the biggest kid in the class. Being with him made me feel less scared.

I soon found out that all the kids in the class were at least one year older than me, but a couple of kids, like Augie, were actually two years older. Maybe two years isn't much of a difference when one of you is thirty-six and the other is thirty-eight, but it's pretty big when you're in grade five. I thought of it not in terms of age but in terms of percentage. If I was nine and they were ten or eleven years old, they were between ten and twenty percent older than me—and that was a lot of percent.

I soon found out why Augie had started to talk to me. He really didn't know anybody else in our class either. All of the people he'd been with—his friends— had passed at the end of the year and had moved on to grade six. He'd been left behind. He was probably scared too, just in a different way, and he had a different way of showing it. I'd learned that with Augie, sometimes when he acted confident he *was* confident. Other times when he acted confident he was really scared and unsure of himself.

"And you want us to give money . . . to you two?" a boy asked.

"Just a dollar," Augie said. "We need four hundred kids to give us a buck."

"But that's a lot of money," another boy said.

"You need that much to buy a snake?" a girl asked.

"It isn't just a snake," I said. "It's a boa constrictor."

"Will it be as big as the one that was killed?" another girl asked.

"No, that would cost too much. It'll be about half as long and a lot younger," I explained.

"And we need the money soon," Augie explained. "We're hoping to buy the snake this weekend and give it to Mr. Johnston on Monday afternoon, so you have to bring in the money tomorrow, or at least before Friday."

"And where do they bring the money to?" Mr. Yeoman asked.

"Me and Ricky will be in the lobby outside the office at lunch every day until Friday. Just bring the money down to us there."

"And can people make contributions to the fund before that?" Mr. Yeoman asked.

"Sure," I said.

"Good." Mr. Yeoman removed his wallet from his pants and pulled out a five-dollar bill. "Let me be the first in line."

I held open a big brown envelope, and Mr. Yeoman dropped the bill inside. "Thanks a lot."

"I've got some money now too!" a girl said.

"So do I!" another girl piped in.

They came forward and dropped their money in the envelope. I could see that one had dropped in a quarter and the other a dollar. Every quarter helped.

"Is there anything more, boys?" Mr. Yeoman asked.

"Yeah, there is one more thing we should tell everybody. This is all a surprise. Mr. Johnston doesn't know we're doing this." Augie smiled. "When we're in the lobby by the office, we'll be sitting under a big sign that will say *Help Buy New Uniforms for the School Basketball Team*. And the announcements you'll be hearing for the rest of the week will remind you to bring in your money for the new uniforms."

"That's pretty sneaky," Mr. Yeoman said.

"It was Mr. Skully's idea," I said.

Mr. Yeoman said, "Excellent!"

"So we'd like people not to even talk about giving money to buy a snake. We wouldn't want Mr. Johnston to overhear somebody talking in the hall. Just talk about buying new uniforms and everybody in the school will know what you mean."

"Sounds like a well-thought-out plan," Mr. Yeoman

said. "Well, boys, if there's nothing more, you'll have to excuse us so we can get back to our lessons."

"Thanks for the time," Augie said.

Before the door had even closed behind us, we heard Mr. Yeoman start teaching.

"That went pretty good," Augie said as we walked down the hall.

"It did go easier than I thought it would," I admitted.

"I'm glad you thought so. How about if you do most of the talking with the next class?" Augie asked.

"Um . . . I was hoping you could do it."

"Sure, no problem. I'll do the next class and maybe the next few after that."

"Thanks."

"That's okay. We still have seventeen classes to go. There'll be plenty of chances for you to talk too."

Chapter Eleven

"Hi, Ricky, hi, Augie," a girl said as she passed us in the hall at lunch.

"Yeah, hi," I mumbled back. Augie nodded.

That had been happening a lot—people I didn't know at all were saying hello or coming up and talking to me or asking me questions. Augie was used to everybody knowing him, but this was different for me. It made me feel uncomfortable—like, if they knew my name, what else did they know about me?

"How many more classes do we have to do today?" Augie asked.

I pulled a piece of paper out of my back pocket and unfolded it. I looked at all the little check marks to show which classes we'd already done. "We did all the grade sevens yesterday and more than half of the eights. We have"—I ran my finger down the list—"four more classes to do today."

"We can have those done by noon," Augie said.

"That's good. We don't want to miss any more school."

"Speak for yourself. I'd be happy to miss the rest of the week."

"We're not missing anything. We just have to make it up on our own time, like this weekend," I reminded him.

"That doesn't sound so good. Have we missed anything yet?"

"An assignment in English."

"What sort of an assignment?" Augie asked.

"We have to do a paper on friendship."

"Friendship?"

"Yeah, we have to write about somebody who's a friend," I explained.

"Doesn't sound too bad."

"And you have to co-write your paper with somebody."

"So, who was assigned to be my partner? Was it Elyse?" he asked hopefully.

"Afraid not. It's me."

"You? You and I are working together? That's fantastic! So, when is the assignment due?"

"Monday."

"That's pretty soon. I guess we should start working on it—how about Sunday afternoon?"

"I was hoping for sooner."

"We can put it off. This should be a snap," Augie said. "I already know you and you know me, and we're friends, so what could be easier?"

95

"It shouldn't be too hard," I agreed.

"And we're only going to miss a few more classes and then we're done."

"Not quite. We still haven't collected the money."

"That'll happen, starting in a few minutes," Augie said.

"What if nobody shows up?"

"People will come," Augie said. We were on our way to the lobby to start collecting money for the "basketball uniforms."

"What if not enough people come, or they don't bring enough money?" I asked. "What if we only collect half the money we need?"

"Then, we'll buy him half a snake." Augie laughed.

"No, seriously."

"We'll collect enough money. Everybody thinks this is a good idea."

"I wish I could be that confident," I said.

"You're always nervous. You should spend less time worrying about what *might* go *wrong* and think about what *will* go *right*."

"That's easy for you to say," I said.

Of course Augie was right. I could always see all the possible things that could go wrong. It was a double curse—to be nervous enough to imagine all sorts of bad things, and smart enough to know they could come true.

"You know the other great part of all this snake stuff, don't you?" Augie asked.

"What other great part?"

"The first school dance of the year is coming up in just two weeks, and you and I will be able to take almost any girl in the school. All we have to do is ask!"

"I wasn't planning on asking anybody."

"Okay, fine," he said. "No problem."

I looked at him suspiciously. Why wasn't he arguing with me more about this, trying to convince me to ask somebody? That wasn't like Augie at all.

"You don't have to ask anybody," Augie said.

Now I understood what he was doing. "Do you really think that reverse psychology will work on me?" I asked.

"I'm not using any type of psychology. I just know that it doesn't really matter whether you ask anybody or not. Because I know for a fact that somebody will be asking you to the dance."

"You do? Who?" I was pleased and scared all at once.

"I don't know for sure, but I bet lots of girls will ask you. Everybody in the school knows you now, and they think you are 'such a nice boy' for helping Mr. Johnston, that somebody will ask you for sure. Especially once the word gets out."

"What do you mean by that?" I asked.

"I'm just going to mention to a couple of girls that

you really like them, but you're too shy to ask them out and—"

"You wouldn't dare!" I practically yelled.

"Of course I would. It would be doing you a favour and—"

"Don't do me any favours!"

"Fine, suit yourself. If you'd rather sit at home with your animals instead of spending a night with me and Elyse."

"You're going to the dance with Elyse?" I asked in amazement.

"Well, we still have a few details to go over. Things like her knowing that we're going to the dance together . . . but that'll work itself out."

I couldn't help but laugh.

We walked into the front lobby of the school. There, already waiting, was Elyse, sitting under a big sign that read, *Help Buy New Uniforms for the School Basketball Team*. It was a nice sign—Elyse had made it last night and showed it to us this morning when we gave Garfield another treatment.

"I was beginning to think you two weren't going to show up," she said.

I looked at my watch. "We're not supposed to be here for another five minutes."

"That hasn't stopped other people from dropping by," she said.

"Kids have already dropped off money?" I asked.

"Lots. What do you want to do with this?" she asked. Elyse pushed forward a little wooden box overflowing with coins.

"Wow! How much is there?" I exclaimed.

"I'm not completely sure. People just kept coming forward and—"

"Here's my money," a girl said as she dropped a dollar into the box.

"Thank you," Elyse sang out.

Augie pulled the container toward him, sank his hand into the coins and pulled out a fistful of money. "I'll start counting while you two collect," Augie said.

I pulled up a second chair and sat down behind the table, beside Elyse. Augie, meanwhile, had taken the wooden box to the far end of the table. He dumped the money out with a loud clank and clatter and began sorting the coins into piles. I couldn't help but notice the bills.

"It looks like some people are giving more than a dollar," I said to Elyse.

"Some are giving a lot more. There's a twenty-dollar bill in there."

"Wow, I can't imagine any kid giving twenty dollars!" I exclaimed.

Two more kids walked up and gave us a dollar each.

"Thank you," Elyse said as they walked off. "The twenty wasn't from a kid, it was from Mr. Skully."

"Mr. Skully!" I exclaimed.

"Yeah. He seems pretty nice . . . for a vice-principal."

A boy from my class, Frankie, came up to the table and pulled out his wallet. "How's it going?" he asked.

"Pretty good, so far," I answered.

Frankie was one of the biggest kids in the school. And one of the toughest. I'd seen him in a fistfight last year against one of the grade eight kids. Not only did he win, but he won easily. I'd always been really careful around him since then. Luckily we were friends.

Frankie opened up his wallet and turned it upside down. Coins rained out onto the table, bouncing and rolling, a couple of them hitting the floor. He bent down to grab the escaping money and put it back beside the other coins. There were quarters, and dimes, pennies and nickels.

He pushed the pile toward us. "I hope this will help."

"It will, for sure," Elyse said. "But there's a lot more than a dollar here."

"Yeah, there must be . . ." I tried quickly to total the jumble of coins in my head.

"Three dollars and fifty-four cents. I was saving up for something, but I figure Mr. Johnston needs a new snake more than I need another CD."

"Thanks, thanks a lot," Elyse said.

"Let me know if there's anything I can do to help."

"We're okay, but thanks," I said.

"No problem." He started to walk away, but then turned around as if a thought had just hit him. "I hope you're taking good care of the money," Frankie said.

"We're going to."

"Good, 'cause you're collecting a lot, which will make some people pay attention to you. And if something should happen to the cash, you're gonna have a whole lot of other people angry—if you know what I mean."

"I think I understand," I said.

"Good. I don't mind giving money to help Mr. Johnston, but I won't be none too pleased if my money gets lost." He paused and shot me a look to remind me what he was capable of when he wasn't pleased. "I'll see you two in class," he said, and then strolled off.

"What did he mean by that?" Elyse asked.

"He wants us to take good care of the money," I said. "*Good* care."

"That was very nice of him to be concerned," Elyse said.

I guess she wasn't as worried about having Frankie "concerned" as I was. "Frankie's a pretty good guy," I said, mostly to reassure myself.

"Everybody in this school has been so generous," she said. "A couple of girls already gave up their milk money, and one girl said she had money to buy lunch, but brought her lunch instead so she could donate the money, and there's Mr. Skully, and of course you and Augie." She turned and looked at Augie, occupied at the far end of the table, out of ear shot. "I'm almost embarrassed to mention this now," she said. "But I really thought Augie was a jerk."

"Augie! He's not a jerk!" I protested.

"Well, I know that now, but I sure thought so before."

"But, why?"

"You know, he does come on a bit strong. Doing those voices and telling all those bad jokes."

"I like his jokes."

"You would, you're his best friend," she said. "And he always seems to be in trouble."

"He doesn't get in trouble that much," I said.

"And he kept on talking to me all the time," Elyse continued.

"He was just doing that because he likes you and—" I stopped myself too late.

Elyse flashed a little smile.

"He likes *everybody*," I added, trying to undo what I'd done.

Her smile widened. I didn't think she was buying what I was selling.

"Unbelievable," Augie said, returning with the container.

I hoped he hadn't heard what we'd been saying. "What's unbelievable?" I asked.

"I have in my hands . . . one hundred and ninety-one dollars and twenty-three cents."

"Fantastic!" Elyse said.

"And we have another . . . almost ten dollars here," I added.

"That puts us more than halfway to our total, and this is just the first part of the first day," Augie said.

"Hello gentlemen . . . and lady." It was Mr. Johnston.

"Hi, Mr. Johnston," Augie replied, and Elyse and I mumbled greetings, as well.

What was he doing here?

"It looks like you're doing good business."

"Yeah . . . good," I mumbled, as three more kids deposited money on the table and then walked away. They all looked a little uneasy about Mr. Johnston being there.

"Thanks for the contributions to buy new uniforms!" Augie called out.

"It looks like everybody is really getting behind this project. You've already got quite a haul there," Mr. Johnston said.

"Over two hundred dollars," Elyse said.

"I guess school uniforms are pretty expensive," Mr. Johnston said.

"To get good quality," Augie replied. "And we want only the best for our school teams."

I almost laughed out loud. Augie was so quick on his feet.

"And are you limiting yourselves to donations from students, or will you take contributions from teachers, as well?" Mr. Johnston asked.

"No, lots of teachers have chipped in," Augie said.

"Good, then I'd also like to—"

"You can't!" I exclaimed.

"I can't?" he asked.

"Yeah . . . um . . . because," I stammered. It didn't seem right for him to put money toward his own surprise present.

"Because why?" Mr. Johnston asked.

"Because . . . I . . . we think that . . ."

"That you should save your money because we know how much you're going to have to spend to redo your class," Augie said, jumping in to save me.

"That's very considerate of you boys, but it's because of the break-in that I want to contribute even more."

"I don't understand," I said.

"Let me see if I can explain. The police said that the break-in was probably done by somebody familiar with this school."

"Like a student," Augie said.

"Or a former student," Mr. Johnston added. "The police could be wrong, but it certainly makes sense. The robbers knew the classes and where to look for things like equipment and money. And if that's the case, then instead of it being strangers, it was students whom I'd taught who did all that. That thought made it so much worse, and I just started to think over and over again about all the students whom I've taught over the years, and how I tried my best to be a good teacher and—"

"You *are* a good teacher," I said.

"The best," Augie added.

"Thank you, boys. It's just that I felt a little disillusioned about what I do. And now I see the three of you giving up your time to help the school like this, and it just helps to remind me of all the wonderful students I've had the honour of teaching over the years. And I'm not going to let those people—whoever they are—rob me of my good memories." He paused. "Does that make sense?"

"Perfect sense," Augie said. "So, how much do you want to give?"

"I was thinking this amount," Mr. Johnston said, removing twenty dollars from his wallet.

"Thanks, that'll help," Augie said, taking the money from him.

"I'm glad," Mr. Johnston said. "By the way, will you two boys be in class this afternoon?"

"Yeah, we'll be there," I answered.

"Good. We're going to have that test today."

"Today?" Augie exclaimed. His jaw dropped so far it practically hit the table. "Couldn't we have it tomorrow, to give us more chance to study?"

"You've already had extra time. Besides, if you knew it Monday, you'll know it for sure today. See you there this afternoon," Mr. Johnston said as he walked away.

"I'm dead," Augie said quietly.

"What do you mean?" Elyse asked him. "You're the one who explained osmosis to me."

"Yeah, but that doesn't mean I'm going to do well on the test," Augie said. "Being able to talk about it, explain it with words, and putting it down on paper, are two different things."

"He always says that before a test," I said. I looked at my watch. "We still have twenty-five minutes until lunch recess is over. How about while we're sitting here I'll ask the two of you questions about things I think will be on the test. That'll help all three of us study, okay?"

"That sounds like a good idea," Elyse said.

"Sound like a *lifesaving* idea to me," Augie added.

"Great. So let's start off talking about osmosis again," I began.

Chapter Twelve

"I can't believe how much this money weighs," I said, my pockets heavy with coins. "I've never carried around this much money in my life."

"Me neither. It makes me feel a little nervous," Augie said, looking over his shoulder anxiously.

There was nobody in sight. Everybody else had gone home. We'd stopped at Elyse's to treat Garfield again, and then we'd stayed a little longer because her mother wanted us to have an after-school snack. I couldn't help thinking how nice it was to have somebody waiting for you at home . . . somebody to fix you a snack.

"I don't see anybody," Augie said.

I looked back, as well. Up until Augie mentioning it, I hadn't been nervous at all. I just naturally assumed that as long as I was with Augie I'd be okay, that he'd take care of things. One thing I knew for sure was that I didn't want to run into Jimmie Saunders or any of his friends.

"Two hundred and fifty-seven dollars is a lot of money," I said.

"Do you have a safe place to keep it?"

"I've been thinking about it, and I think I have a great place."

"Where?" he asked.

"I don't want to tell you."

"You're going to keep it a secret from *me*?" he asked. He sounded hurt.

"No, you'll know. You'll even help me put it there. It's just that I don't want to tell you about it. I want to show you."

"And it's safe?"

"Safest place I can think to put over two hundred dollars," I said.

"Good," Augie answered, again looking around to see if anybody was following us or could hear what we said. "Now, let's not talk about it, okay?"

I shrugged. "Fine with me. How do you think you did on the science test?"

"Ugh . . . now there's something else I don't want to talk about. I blew it," he said, shaking his head.

"You couldn't have."

"I did. I'm almost positive I did."

"But you knew all the stuff, all the answers, when I asked you questions at lunch. You couldn't just lose it in forty minutes."

"I didn't lose it. I still know the answers. If you asked me right now, I could tell you everything you'd ever want to know about cell biology," he said.

"I don't understand. You knew it, then forgot it, and

now you remember it again?"

"I didn't forget it, I just couldn't get it out on the paper. That's just the way it is."

"But that doesn't make any sense," I argued. "Maybe you're just nervous about it and you really did better than you think you did."

"I'd rather you were right than me, but I don't think so."

We turned the corner to my street and I could see my house up ahead.

"Come on, tell me where you're going to keep the money," Augie asked.

I knew that not knowing bothered him. "I'll give you a little hint."

"Great, just what I need, another test to see how smart I'm not. Go ahead and give me a hint."

"Okay. Where do pirates keep their treasure?" I asked.

"Is this like a joke, like Inuit keep their cash in a snowbank?" Augie asked.

"No, seriously."

"I don't know . . . on their ship . . . um, under their bed . . . in a treasure chest . . . buried with an X marking the spot."

"Exactly!"

"Exactly, what?"

"We're going to bury it," I said.

"Are you crazy!" he exclaimed. "We can't just dig a

hole in your backyard and bury the money!"

"Who said anything about my backyard?" I asked. "Or even outside."

I took my house key from around my neck.

"Wait here," I said, putting the key in the lock.

Hearing the noise, Candy started to howl, and I could hear her charging down the hall, finally slamming into the door with a loud *thud*.

"It's just me, girl!" I called out. "It's okay," I said as I squeezed in the door.

Candy jumped up on me excitedly, her tail wagging, her tongue flicking out, trying to lick my face.

"Have you been a good girl?" I asked, petting her behind the ears, then pushing her back down to the ground. She followed closely behind, bouncing up on me as I walked through the house to the back door and opened it up so she could go outside for a pee. She bounded out the door, getting no more than two steps before she spied three of my squirrels on the grass in the back corner of the yard. She bellowed loudly as she jumped down the steps and charged across the yard!

"Candy, leave them alone!"

The squirrels scurried up the closest tree long before the dog could close the gap between them. Candy, going full speed, tried to stop, but instead crashed head-first into the trunk.

"Stupid dog," I muttered. I closed the door and went back to get Augie off the front porch.

"So, have you got it figured out yet?" I asked as I let Augie in through the front door.

"I've got nothing figured out except that I know if I was a robber, there's no way I'd ever break into your house with that dog around."

"Candy's a good watch dog, but I've got something even better," I said. "Come with me."

I went up the stairs. My sister's cat—the only one precious enough to be indoors—came out of her room and stared at me. It was funny how I liked every animal in the whole world except for this one. I opened the door to my room and Augie followed behind.

"We're going to hide the money in my room," I said.

"Then, what were you talking about when you said you were going to bury it?"

"I am."

"In here?" he asked.

I nodded.

"Where?"

"There," I said, pointing to my alligator's pen.

"With the alligator?"

"Would you want to put your hand in there?" I asked.

"Not if I wanted to keep it," he admitted. "But how?"

I pulled an old metal cookie tin out from under my bed. "We put the money in here, put the lid back on, and then we bury it in the sand in Ollie's pen."

"You're joking . . . right?"

I started to pull the money from my pockets and drop it into the tin. "Can you think of anyplace safer?" I asked.

"Maybe tied around your dog's neck."

"That's a close second," I admitted as I took out the last of the bills. "Empty your pockets and put the money in here," I said, handing him the tin.

I leaned over the pen and looked down at Ollie. He was, as he almost always was, in the water. He was sleeping on the bottom, his eyes closed. Off to the side, the light flickering off their scales, a few minnows swam around the rocks. I counted three. I'd put six in there that morning before I'd left for school. I knew where the other three were, and why Ollie was sleeping. I always felt like sleeping after lunch too.

I reached in and started to scoop away sand from the farthest corner of the pen. The sand was about four inches deep, and I needed to clear it away right to the bottom. I began thinking that maybe I should have used some sort of shovel. Occasionally my sister's cat used the pen as a litter box, and I wasn't crazy about uncovering some treasure that he'd deposited in there.

Of course, the worst thing about that stupid cat using Ollie's pen as a toilet was the possibility that Ollie might use the cat as a snack. Sooner or later he'd catch the cat with its pants down and leap out and remove a patch of fur and flesh, and then my sister would go ballistic. All the other animals in the house were my pets. Gandalf was hers. He was a special breed, a Russian Blue. She'd bought him at a pet store, and he'd cost more than two hundred dollars! I couldn't believe that anybody would spend that much money on a cat but that's how she wanted to spend her first pay cheque. You could get all the cats you wanted for free by just walking out into the alley and opening up a can of tuna.

"It's all in there," Augie said, handing me the can.

I took it from him and tapped the lid into place. Next, I placed it in the hole I'd dug. It fit in nicely. I covered it over with a thin layer of sand, spreading the rest out so that there wasn't even a hint that anything was buried there.

"Well?" I asked.

"You're a genius," Augie said. "Maybe we should celebrate your genius by going out and playing some road hockey."

"I don't have time. I have to take care of all the animals, and then we can have a cup of tea while I—"

"Peel some potatoes for supper," Augie said, completing my sentence.

"Yeah."

"Don't you ever have anything else for supper?" he asked.

"I like potatoes. They go with everything," I said. What I didn't say was that it was one of the few things my father knew how to cook.

"Well, I think I can find better things to do than

watch you peel potatoes. I have to get going. I'll see you tomorrow. Try to be on time, okay?"

"I'll try."

I stood at the front window, staring up the street as far as I could see. Nothing. I turned around and looked at the clock on the wall. It was five thirty-seven. My father was seven minutes late. That was hardly late at all. At least once a week he was ten or even twelve minutes late. It wasn't his fault. I knew he tried his best to get home on time. He knew how much I worried. It was just that there were lots of reasons he could be a little late. There was probably a lot of traffic, or maybe there was a stalled car on the highway, or maybe his car had a flat tire, or maybe he had to take care of something at work at the last minute, or there was an accident . . . maybe he was in an accident . . . he was always telling me what a battle zone the highway was . . . .

"Don't be stupid!" I told myself.

I looked at the clock again. Five thirty-nine. Two minutes later. I knew he'd be here soon. In a minute or two. There was nothing to worry about. I saw a car at the end of the street. It looked like our car. He was home! Then it turned into a driveway partway up the street. I felt like a punctured balloon, all the hope leaking out of me.

I ran back into the kitchen. The potatoes were simmering away on the back burner of the stove, a little puff of steam escaping around the lid. I turned the burner down another notch.

The table was already set. I'd put out three settings, even though my sister probably wouldn't be home for dinner. Ever since she'd started working as a secretary at that big company downtown, she missed more than half of our suppers. Lots of times she had extra work to do and she had to stay late. Other times she just stayed downtown and took in a movie or ate dinner at a restaurant with her friends. She said she never wanted to eat another boiled potato for the rest of her life. I liked boiled potatoes.

I went back to the front window. I was sure he was just going to be pulling into the driveway and—he wasn't there. I anxiously looked at the clock again. He was now twelve minutes late. He was almost never that late. I felt my heart start to race and my stomach felt uneasy.

"Where is he?" I asked myself. "He should be home by now."

I tried to think who I should call or what I should do. There was nobody and nothing. I just had to wait. And it wouldn't be long . . . I knew that . . . his car would soon appear at the top of the street . . . maybe not the next car, but within the next three for sure.

Another car turned onto the street. It was little and

red and looked nothing like our big, battered, blue Buick. I was glad it was so different. At least I hadn't gotten my hopes up for nothing.

A second car pulled onto the street. Maybe it could be . . . it wasn't him. That meant that he had to be the next one . . . he had to be. If it wasn't him, then what had happened to him?

"He's okay!" I shouted.

Candy jumped up from the floor where she'd been sleeping, disturbed by my outburst. She came over to my side, wagging her tail.

"It's okay, girl," I said quietly, reaching down to pat her head. "He'll be here soon. You have nothing to worry about."

Candy seemed convinced. She flopped down to the floor and turned over on her back with her paws in the air.

"No matter what happens, girl, you know I'll always be here to take care of you," I said.

I bent down and scratched her tummy. Sometimes I thought how easy it would be to be a dog. Nothing to worry about, nothing to think about.

I started to think things through. What would I do if he didn't come home . . . if he never came home? If he was dead, then it was just Janice and me. She was old enough to take care of herself, but she wasn't old enough to take care of me . . . even if she wanted to. I figured I'd stay until after the funeral. I never got to go to my mother's because I was too young. And then right after that I'd leave. I had my sleeping bag and the tent I bought last summer, and I could fill my knapsack with things, and then just get on my bike and go. Candy would come with me and we would find a place to pitch the tent. There was a clearing in the middle of the woods where practically nobody ever went. We could live there. And I could go to school and get some sort of job so I could earn enough money to buy food and—

I heard the sound of tires against gravel. I stood up and looked out the window in time to see my father's car pull to a stop in our driveway. He was home!

I quickly moved away from the window. My father said he didn't like me to stand there at the window, worrying, just because he was a few minutes late. Anyway, I had things to take care of. I had to drain the potatoes, and put out the meat, and pour us something to drink, and . . . thank you, God . . . thank you.

Chapter Thirteen

I could hear the TV from downstairs. I knew it wasn't that loud—my father always tried to keep it low after I'd gone to bed—but sounds always seem to travel farther at night. If I lay perfectly still and strained my ears, I could make out some of what was being said. Especially the commercials. They were always louder.

I didn't know what time it was but I did know it was late. At least eleven-thirty, maybe later. I'd been in bed, or at least in my bedroom, since just before ten o'clock. I couldn't sleep. So what else was new?

I'd spent some time doing what I always did when I couldn't get to sleep. I'd watched my animals and played with them. Most of them, especially the rodents, like the mice and hamsters and gerbils, were more active at night anyway. Others, like the squirrels, just wanted to sleep. I'd taken down the back of their nesting box and seen them all curled up together in one black ball: the heads and bodies and feet and tails of six squirrels all wrapped around each other so I couldn't see where any one of them started or stopped. They looked peaceful together. It would have been nice to sleep that way. Sleep . . . I wasn't even feeling close to being able to sleep.

I rolled out of my bed and moved across the floor toward the door. I inched out into the hall and stopped at the top of the stairs. The door to my sister's room was closed. There was no light visible under the door and I was sure she was asleep. Sleep was practically all she ever did at home these days. Ever since she'd gotten that job downtown she was always out—working or travelling to work or spending time with her friends or boyfriend. It was like she hardly lived here anymore.

I could hear the TV a lot more clearly here. It was the *Tonight Show* with Jay Leno. I liked Leno. He seemed like a regular guy, like he could live up the street, the sort of neighbour who would help somebody out if they needed something. I could make out a few words, but not enough to understand what he was saying.

Carefully I crept down the stairs, avoiding the eleventh and then the eighth steps, which always creaked. I reached the bottom and sat on the very first step. From there, by craning my neck, I could see the television—and my father. He was sitting in his chair, a laundry basket at his feet, folding clothes. Beside him, on the coffee table, sat a teapot in a cosy, a cup and a piece of toast. He laughed at one of Jay's jokes, but I didn't get it. My father poured himself a cup of tea, and steam rose into the air. He took a sip and went back to folding the laundry.

It was late, but it didn't surprise me to see my father still working. He always seemed to be working. My sister and I helped—we did more work around the house than any other kids I knew—but there was always so much to be done. Cooking, dishes, cleaning, buying groceries, laundry, yardwork, paying bills—and those were just the things he had to do after working all day in a warehouse on the other side of the city.

"Wouldn't you be more comfortable here on the couch?" my father called out.

I smiled—so much for being sneaky. I stood up and joined him in the living room.

"Do you want some tea?" he asked.

"That would be nice."

I walked into the kitchen and took a mug from the counter where they were drying. I grabbed the sugar bowl and brought it back with me. My father liked his with just a little milk. I liked sugar. The more sugar, the better the tea. Four heaping spoonfuls.

"Are you sure you don't want some tea with that sugar?" my father asked.

"I'm trying to cut back a little," I said as I poured in the milk. "Who are his guests tonight?"

"Some singer I don't know and a comedian I haven't heard of either."

It really didn't matter to me who was on the show. I

hardly ever knew who they were. I just liked being here—on the couch—watching with my father. Maybe he didn't stop working, even this late, but at least he slowed down a bit.

"So . . . anything interesting happening at school?"

"You know, the snake thing."

"Oh, yeah, that's right. Anything else?"

"I'm trying out for the basketball team."

"You'll make it," he said. "You're a good player."

"I'm okay," I said. I didn't think he'd ever even seen me play. But it wasn't his fault. Even when the games were after school, he couldn't get there on time from work. Besides, if he ever did get home early, he would have a hundred things to do around the house.

"Your marks holding up?"

"They're good."

"What about art?"

It was the only B on my interim report card. The rest were either an A or an A+.

"I'm trying to improve it," I said.

"Trying isn't enough. You have to bring your mark up. No choice."

"I'll do it."

"To get a scholarship to a good university, you need top marks. I'm working in a warehouse so that you never need to. Understand?"

"I understand."

"Good. You want some of my toast?" he asked.

"Thanks," I said as I reached out and took one of the pieces. It was cold and hard, but that didn't matter either.

"Stretch out there on the couch," he said. "You can stay up until I finish the laundry, and then we'd *both* better get to bed. It's getting late."

I took a bite from the toast and a sip from my tea, and then lay down on the couch. I knew I'd be asleep within a few minutes. I also knew my father would then carry me upstairs, and I'd wake up in my own bed in the morning. I closed my eyes and let the *Tonight Show* guest sing me to sleep.

Chapter Fourteen

"I still can't believe we got all the money so fast," Augie said.

"It is pretty amazing. Three days to raise four hundred dollars," I said.

"I thought we got more than that."

"We did. Twenty-three dollars more," I admitted.

"And what are we going to do with that?"

"I thought we could buy something else for the class. Maybe some turtles."

"That would be nice," Augie said. "You want me to carry the money for a while?"

"I'm okay." The money was still inside the cookie tin, which was inside the plastic grocery bag I was carrying.

"You seem a lot more relaxed about the money," I commented.

"I am," Augie agreed.

"How come?"

"I just started to think about it. Who in their right mind would figure the two of us would be carrying around over four hundred bucks, in a cookie tin, in a shopping bag?"

"I guess you're right," I agreed as I sat down on the bench at the bus stop.

"What I still don't understand, though, is why do we have to go halfway across the city to get this snake."

"Because you can't just go down to the pet store at the mall and get a snake."

"I've seen exotic animals in the mall pet store," Augie said. "Lizards, tarantulas, and I'm sure I've seen a boa in one of the aquariums at the back."

"They have a boa," I admitted. "But not a good one."

"What do you mean, not a good one?"

"It just doesn't look . . . I don't know . . . right."

"It didn't look right?" Augie asked in disbelief. "I'm taking a two-hour bus ride because you don't think the snake looks pretty enough?"

"I didn't say pretty. I said it doesn't look *right*. If the colour is wrong, then maybe it isn't healthy. We don't want to give him a sick snake, do we?"

"I guess not. Here comes the bus," Augie said.

The bus slowed down and pulled over to let us on. We deposited our tokens and wobbled down the aisle as it pulled back into traffic. We sat down at the very back.

"So, where are we going again?" Augie asked.

"It's called Reptile World. It's a special type of pet

store. Nothing furry or cute. The only mammals in the whole place are things like mice and rats."

"Why only mice and rats?"

"Well, you wouldn't want to feed a puppy or a kitten to a snake or alligator, would you?" I asked. "That's what they use the rodents for—reptile chow."

"So all they have is reptiles?" Augie asked in disbelief.

"Yep. Scorpions, tarantulas, all sorts of snakes, iguanas, Gila monsters, and alligators and caiman. That's where I got Ollie from. They have over two dozen alligators, including one that's almost nine feet long."

"Who would buy a nine-foot alligator?" Augie asked.

"Nobody. That's why it's that big. He was once a little guy, but nobody ever bought him. So now he's sort of like the store's mascot."

"Say," Augie said, "I never really thought about it, but your alligator is still growing, right?"

"Of course. He's twice as big as when I got him."

"So what are you going to do with him when he gets to be as big as the one at the store?" Augie asked.

I'd been thinking about that myself. Nine feet long was maybe ten years away, but even a four-foot gator was more than I ever wanted to share a bedroom with. "I'll think of something," I said with a shrug. "Maybe I'll give it to you as a birthday present."

"Funny."

I wanted to change the subject. "I called and they

told me there are over two dozen boa constrictors in stock, so we'll be able to pick out a good one."

"We'll take any one you want. You're the expert. I'll be happy as long as I don't have to handle them."

"But you like snakes," I protested.

"No, I don't. They give me the creeps."

"But I've seen you holding Bogart. You used to hold him and—"

"And did you ever notice when I did that?" Augie asked.

I shook my head.

"When the girls in the class were around. I didn't want them to think I was a wimp or nothing. Can you honestly say that you *like* snakes?" he asked.

"They're interesting animals."

"Yeah, but that's not what I asked."

"Well . . . they're not my favourite," I admitted. "But they are Mr. Johnston's, and that's what's important. Speaking of Mr. Johnston . . . I still don't know how you didn't do better on that test."

"Hey, I'm happy. I passed it."

"But just barely. You know that stuff really well. You know it better than a sixty-two percent."

"Sixty-two isn't bad . . . for me. I'm okay with that mark."

"But maybe Mr. Johnston would let you take it again, and you could get better than that."

"Or worse. I don't think it matters if I write the test

one more time or ten more times, I'm not going to get much better than a sixty-two."

"But if you—"

"Maybe *you* should rewrite the test," Augie suggested.

"Me? I got a ninety-four!"

"But you could have done better. You could have got perfect," Augie said.

"Perfect would be good, but I'm happy with my mark—"

"And so am I," Augie said. "So let's drop it, okay?"

I nodded. Maybe he was happy with it. But I knew he could do better. And so did Mr. Johnston. He and I had had a talk after class today. I'd told him how Augie knew all the things when we talked to him, and how sometimes he just didn't put down what he knew. Mr. Johnston said that was interesting and he wanted to try an experiment. He was going to give Augie an oral test. Ask the questions and let Augie "talk" the answers. I didn't know how Augie would feel about being an experiment, but I knew he'd get over it if his mark shot up.

Reptile World was very different from any other pet store I'd been to in my whole life. My father had driven me here about a year ago when we'd bought Ollie.

Rather than being in the mall, with cute little kittens and puppies in display cases in the front windows, it was located in an industrial plaza, set back from the road. If you didn't know where it was, you would miss the sign above the door of the store.

"This place smells like your bedroom," Augie said when we walked in.

"Gee, thanks."

I would have argued, but I knew he wasn't saying that to hurt my feelings. It was true. There was a kind of musty, almost swampy smell. I knew how to get rid of it—change the water in Ollie's pen every day. I also knew that I liked my fingers more than I disliked the smell. The alligator pit here was located in the back corner of the store, and I figured they weren't any more anxious to change the water there than I was to change Ollie's.

"I don't like the look of those," Augie said, gesturing to some small signs posted on the wall, just inside the door. The first one said, *Shoplifters will be eaten.* The second read, *Not responsible for missing possessions or fingers . . . DON'T reach into pens!*, while the last one had bold lettering that stated, *Watch your children—alligators don't like to share!*

"At least you can't say they didn't warn you," I said. "Come on, the snakes are over this way."

We walked down aisles filled with glass aquariums and terrariums. Each held a different species or size of reptile. I wanted to stop and stare at the amazing collection of creatures, but I knew we didn't have much time. Augie said he had to be back home by two o'clock because he had to go somewhere with his family. I headed straight to the snake area.

Even if I hadn't known where it was, it still would have been easy to locate. Suspended from the ceiling, coiled and wrapped around a fake tree branch, was a gigantic snake. It was made out of plastic, or rubber or something, and the whole thing was suspended from the ceiling by wire. It was an exact model of the largest anaconda ever recorded. From end to end it was over thirty feet long.

I stopped in the middle of the floor, surrounded on all sides by glass pens—some almost as big as my whole bedroom—filled with all types of snakes. Some cages held more than one type. I knew it was important which ones, and which sizes, shared space. Different types of constrictors—snakes that squeeze their prey—can be together, as long as they are roughly the same size. But those that are different, even if they are the same type, have to be separated so the big ones don't eat the small ones.

"Why would somebody want one of these as a pet?" Augie asked. He was standing in front of a pen holding a large hooded cobra—one of the most deadly poisonous snakes in the world.

I shook my head. "I don't know. Lots of people

would think that somebody would have to be crazy to keep a boa constrictor."

"Or an alligator," Augie added with a smile.

"Or an alligator," I agreed. "But some people keep rattlesnakes and cobras as pets. I heard you can get the poison gland removed."

"And then they can't bite you?" Augie asked.

"No, they can still bite you; they just don't inject poison when they bite."

"Oh, that's better."

"It is," I said. "Do you want to hear a story?"

"Will it gross me out?" Augie asked.

"Probably. You know that rattlesnakes live in places like deserts, right?"

"If you say so."

"And deserts are really hot in the day, but get cold at night."

"Yeah."

"And because snakes, like all reptiles, are cold-blooded they need to find someplace warm to sleep at night."

"Yeah."

"So some people go camping in the desert, and they sleep in a nice warm snugly sleeping bag."

"I don't think I like where this is going," Augie said.

I smiled. "And in the middle of the night, while they're sleeping, the rattlesnake comes gliding along and slips down into the sleeping bag along with them."

"Aww," Augie said, shuddering.

"Can you imagine waking up in the morning and feeling something moving around in the bottom of your sleeping bag?"

Augie didn't say a word, but the look of disgust on his face said everything.

"And as long as you don't move, you're okay, the rattlesnake won't bite you. So you have to lie there . . . maybe for an hour . . . maybe for two hours . . . not moving, and then wait until the rattlesnake finally decides to leave. You can feel it starting to slide up the side of your body, moving to the opening in the sleeping bag, and then popping out, right by your face, and gliding away," I said as I moved my arm, snake-like, up past Augie's face.

"I'm *never* going to go camping," Augie said.

"You've got nothing to worry about. There isn't a rattlesnake of that type within a thousand kilometres of Toronto—other than in people's houses as pets."

"I'm starting to think I like constrictors better all the time," Augie said.

"And they're really not that dangerous, at least until they get to be that size," I said, gesturing to the ceiling.

"Is that life-size?" Augie asked.

I nodded. "Full-grown anaconda."

"More like death-size, if you ask me," Augie said. "Can you imagine that thing creeping up on you?"

"They don't usually sneak up on you," I said.

"Mostly they sit up in trees, like that one, and then they just drop down on top of you."

Augie shuddered slightly and then took a couple of steps backward so he was no longer directly underneath the model. I had to admit to myself that even I wanted to take a step backward.

"You don't have to worry about him," a voice said behind us.

Augie and I turned around to see a thin man with long stringy hair that looked like it hadn't been washed in a while. On his chest was a badge that identified him as a staff person.

"But if he was real," he continued, "I'd advise you to move really quick before he dropped on you. Do you know how they eat people?" he asked.

"Whole. Headfirst," I answered.

"That's right!" he said, sounding both surprised and happy. "Guess you know a little bit about snakes."

"I know some," I said.

"Most people are pretty ignorant about snakes. If you have any questions, I can answer them," he said. "If not, feel free to just browse."

"We're not here to browse," Augie said. "We're here to buy a snake."

"These snakes cost a whole lot of money," the man said, gesturing to the snakes in the surrounding pens.

"We have a lot of money," Augie said.

"I'm talking hundreds of dollars," the salesman said.

"We *have* hundreds of dollars. Four hundred," Augie said.

"On you? Here?" the man asked.

Augie reached out and took the bag from my hand. "Right here," he said, holding out the bag. "Four hundred and twenty-three dollars."

"Are your parents here with you?" he asked.

"No, we came on the bus," I answered.

"And they're okay about you doing this?"

"Sure . . . yeah . . . why wouldn't they be?" I asked.

"It's just that lots of parents, especially mothers, don't like their kids to have pet snakes. Your mother is okay about this?" he asked, looking directly at me.

"She's fine with—"

"We're not going to keep it at either of our houses," Augie said. "It's for our school . . . for our teacher."

"Your teacher?" the man said, a confused look on his face. "Are you two boys from Osler Senior Public School?"

"Yeah, we are," I said, wondering how he could know that.

"And your teacher is Grant Johnston, right?"

I didn't know about the Grant part, but Johnston was right. Augie and I nodded in agreement.

"And that money in your bag is from every kid in your school," he added.

"Yeah, it is . . . but how do you know?" I asked.

"The reptile world isn't that big, even in a city as

large as Toronto. We heard all about it. The break-in, what happened to the boa constrictor, the school getting behind it and raising money to buy him a new one. Are you the two boys responsible for all this?"

"Us and a girl who helped collect the money," I said.

"Then, I want to shake your hands," the man said as he grabbed first my hand and then Augie's, shaking them enthusiastically. I felt embarrassed, and more than a little goofy.

"We heard about it all," he said. "How much money did you say you had raised?"

"Over four hundred dollars," I said.

"Four hundred and *twenty-three* dollars," Augie corrected.

"And you want a boa constrictor," the man said.

"To replace his boa."

"Of course," he said. "Well, four hundred dollars—I mean, four hundred and twenty-three dollars would get you any of the boas in this terrarium here," he said, pointing to a small glass pen beside him. There were three or four boas visible amongst the branches and foliage.

"But those are so tiny," Augie said.

"The largest in there is just over two feet long."

Augie turned to me. "I thought you said that four hundred bucks could buy us a three-footer?"

"I thought it could," I said, caught unawares and feeling suddenly like I'd done something wrong.

"It could have, a year or so ago," the man said.

It had been over a year since I'd been there. How was I to know that the prices had gone up?

"I guess that's the best we can do," I said. "The important thing is that it's healthy."

"But we were really hoping that we could get him a bigger snake," Augie said.

"And you can," the man said.

"I don't understand," I said.

"I'm in charge of this department and I'm not selling you anything at the retail cost," the man said.

That didn't clear up anything for me.

"You mean you're going to sell us a snake wholesale?" Augie asked.

The man smiled and nodded.

I still didn't understand. "What does that mean?" I asked.

Augie smiled. "It's sales talk, stuff I know from my parents' store. It means that instead of selling to us at the cost the store normally charges to customers, he's going to charge us the price they pay when they *buy* a snake."

"So . . . you're not going to charge us four hundred dollars?" I asked, still feeling confused.

"Oh, no, I'm still going to charge you four hundred dollars. But for that four hundred dollars I'm going to sell you a lot more snake."

"You mean . . . ?"

He gestured to the pens behind him. "There are three snakes in there. One is five-and-a-half feet long, the second just over six feet and the biggest is close to seven feet. Whichever of the three boas you want . . . it's yours for four hundred and twenty-three dollars."

Chapter Fifteen

Augie and I sat at the very back of the bus. Between us, inside a large burlap bag tied at the top, was the snake. The bus was crowded and there were a few people standing. A couple of people had eyed us, annoyed that we were taking up a seat with our luggage, but I just didn't like the thought of the heavy snake moving around inside the bag on my lap. Besides, as long as it was left alone and undisturbed, it wasn't going to move much, and that was good. I had a pretty good idea how the other passengers and the driver would react if they found we had a six-foot snake on board.

"I couldn't believe how the snake reacted when that guy grabbed it," Augie said.

"It was a little . . . wild, wasn't it?" I agreed.

The snake had put up a good fight. The salesman had gone into the pen to get it, and the boa had twisted and twirled and fought, trying first to get away from him, and then to get out of his grasp. He had carried it out, and then it took both Augie and me to help him put it into the burlap sack. I wasn't expecting it to be like that. I just thought that all boas were like Bogart, sort of easygoing and relaxed. He said that since it hadn't been handled very much, it wasn't used to people. It certainly wasn't like Bogart at all, and I even had second thoughts about buying it, but he explained that it would become a lot better when it was being held all the time. He said not to worry. I was worried, but I believed him.

Augie stood up and grabbed the pull cord that ran above the windows. He tugged on it and a bell rang to signal to the driver that we wanted out at the next stop. I got up, too, and grabbed the burlap sack. I felt the weight and struggled to lift it while moving between the people, holding onto the poles, trying to fight against the rocking and rolling of the bus.

"Excuse me," I said as I bumped against a woman who was rushing to take my seat.

"You should be more careful," she scolded as she squeezed by me and plopped down.

"I'm sorry—"

"She bumped into *you*," Augie said. "She should be apologizing to you!"

"Watch your manners, young man," she said sharply.

"I would have watched yours, if you had any," Augie snapped back. "You're just lucky this is our stop . . . or I'd show you what's in the bag."

"Augie, come on!" I pleaded. I had already made my way to the steps of the back doorway, and the bus was slowing down.

Augie chuckled, and joined me on the step as the bus came to a stop and the door popped open. I practically jumped out onto the sidewalk, with Augie right on my heels. As the bus started to pull away, I could see the woman scowling at us through the back window. Augie brought his hand up to his mouth and, with dramatic flair, blew her a kiss. Her expression changed to shock and then anger.

"You shouldn't have done that," I said.

"Why not? She was rude."

"But we could have got in trouble."

"Trouble? What was she going to do, jump off the bus and chase us down? It's no big deal. We have more important things to figure out. Like, have you figured out where you're going to keep the snake?"

"Not exactly."

"Well, we have to think of something. Could you just leave it in the burlap bag for the weekend?"

"Nope, and could you give me a hand with this? It's heavy," I said.

"Sure." Augie grabbed a corner of the bag, relieving me of some of the weight.

"It wouldn't be good for the snake to be in the bag all weekend. I was also thinking that it might be able to work its way out, somehow," I said. "I'm going to have to build something."

"Like what?"

"My father has lots of wood in the basement, and he

has all sorts of tools. I've made most of the pens in my room," I said.

"And you can build something in the next hour or so?"

"Well, I have the rest of the day, and you could help and . . ." Then I remembered that Augie had to be home within the next hour because he had to go out with his family.

"Do you think you could skip going out with your family?" I asked. "I could really use another pair of hands."

Augie was next to useless with a saw or hammer, but what I really wanted, more than his assistance in building, was his company. I didn't want to be alone with the snake. It was big—bigger than I'd ever imagined we'd get—and I was feeling unnerved.

"Believe me, I wish I could stay, but I can't. It's special. My father is even closing down the store three hours early."

"Where are you going that's so important?" I asked.

"There's this thing happening at the synagogue."

"At the what?"

"The synagogue. Our church."

"But it's Saturday," I said. "Why are you going to church on a Saturday? Is somebody getting married?"

"We always go on Saturdays," Augie said.

"No, you don't. Your father's store is always open

Saturdays, and you're with me most of the time."

"That's when we are *supposed* to go . . . you know, my *people*."

"You have people?" I asked. This was getting more confusing.

"No, of course not! I mean people that are the same religion as me."

"What religion is that?" I asked.

"You don't know?"

"No," I said, shaking my head. "That's why I asked."

"My name is Levy . . . Augie Levy."

"I know your name."

"Well, it's just, you know . . . that's a Jewish name. I'm Jewish. My family is Jewish. How could you not know that?"

"I don't know. It just never came up. You never mentioned it."

"I just thought you'd know. We've been friends for three years," he said.

"I know how long we've been friends, I just didn't know what religion you were."

"Sometimes you amaze me," he said.

He had that tone of voice he used when he thought I'd done or said something stupid.

"Big deal," I said, defending myself. "I bet you don't know what religion I am!"

"Sure I do," he said. "You're . . . you're not Jewish."

"I didn't ask you what I *wasn't*. What *am* I?"

"I don't know," he admitted sheepishly. "I didn't even know you went to church."

"I don't, but if I did, I'd go to the one at the end of my street."

"So that means you're Presba . . . Presba . . ."

"Presbyterian."

"But if you don't go, how can you be anything?" Augie asked.

"I've been before."

"When?" he asked.

"A while ago," I admitted, looking down at the ground. "When I was small."

"And you used to go a lot?"

"Not a lot—just once."

Augie burst into laughter. "You've only been to church once? Compared to you I'm downright religious. We sometimes go to synagogue *twice a year*."

"And it wasn't even my idea to go in the first place. My father said it would be good for me, so he sent me."

"And what happened?" Augie asked.

"They put all us kids in the basement. We had to go to Sunday School."

"More school?"

I knew by the tone of Augie's voice that he was shocked. The thought of going to school even five days a week was more than he could bear.

"There was a teacher and she was explaining about Jesus and stuff. It was awful."

"Why, you always do well in school," Augie said.

"Not this one."

"What happened?"

"It was crowded, and we were sitting on the floor, and it was hot, really hot ... and I didn't know anybody. And when it was almost over they gave us chocolate milk to drink. Warm chocolate milk."

As I said the words I could almost taste that sour, warm, chocolate milk in my mouth and feel it going into my gut and churning all around.

"I still don't know what's so bad about that," Augie said.

"I threw up ... in church ... on the minister."

Augie shrieked with laughter and almost dropped his end of the bag.

"I'm glad you find it so funny."

"I do!" he exclaimed. "Even *you* have to admit it's funny."

"Well ..."

Augie pretended to throw up, and I started to laugh along with him.

"Okay, so it's funny," I admitted as we came up to my house. "And you know, to this day, I've never been back to church ... or drunk chocolate milk."

Augie started to laugh even harder.

"If you're almost through laughing, maybe we can go inside. You wait on the porch with the snake."

"Are you going to put Candy away?" Augie asked.

"That, and find out if my sister is home."

"How come?"

"She's not crazy about snakes. If she's home, we have to sneak it in."

"Sneak in fifty pounds worth of boa constrictor?" Augie asked in amazement, gesturing to the burlap sack.

"If you don't think we can do it, you can always take the snake home to your place," I suggested.

"You've got to be . . ." Augie paused. "You *are* joking, right?"

"Of course. Wait here."

I unlocked the door and started to turn the handle. I heard Candy begin to howl. The barking got louder, and I could hear the pounding of her feet on the floor as she reached the door before I could even fully open it.

"It's okay, girl, it's just me," I said to her as I squeezed in.

She leaped up on me, and I grabbed her collar with one hand while I scratched her behind the ear with the other.

"I'm home!" I called out as I dragged Candy down the hall. "Hello!" There was no answer.

I went into the kitchen. There was a note taped to the fridge: *Gone grocery shopping. Be back by 2:30, Dad.*

My father not being home meant less explaining to do. Once an animal was actually in the house, Dad never complained. But it also meant that I didn't have him around to give me advice about the pen I was going to build. He was a carpenter and an expert with wood, and tools and building things. Then again, I only needed it to work for a couple of days, so how good did it have to be?

I pulled and pushed Candy into the living room. I motioned for her to jump up on the chesterfield, which she did willingly. She never needed a second invitation to get on the furniture. I then closed the door behind me as I left. I hurried to the front door where Augie and the snake were waiting.

"What took you so long?" Augie demanded.

"I was only gone for a couple of minutes."

"It seemed longer than that. I didn't like being alone with the snake. It started moving around . . . a lot."

I looked down at the sack sitting on the floor of the porch. The bag was undulating and quivering as the snake moved around inside.

"I'm just glad you're keeping it at your house," Augie said.

I didn't answer. Up until now, I hadn't even thought about the snake being anywhere else—not that there was anyplace else to keep it—but now I didn't feel so sure about the whole thing. It was a snake—a big snake. Maybe not big enough to hurt me, well, at least not kill me, but it could kill other things in my house. Things like my squirrels, or one of the cats. And a six-foot boa constrictor could easily overpower a small dog, even a dog as mean as Candy.

What had I gotten myself into? Did I really want a six-foot boa constrictor in my house?

"We'd better hurry up," Augie said. Before I could say something, he grabbed the bag, picked it up and walked into the house. "Are we going up to your room?"

"Nope, the basement."

"And is your dog locked away someplace so I can walk to the basement without getting bit?" Augie asked.

"You're okay," I reassured him. "She's behind closed doors."

As we moved down the hall, Candy started barking loudly and scratching furiously against the door, like she was trying to dig her way through.

"What have I ever done to that dog to make her hate me like that?" Augie asked.

"Nothing. She hates everybody. Come on."

I switched on the lights and started down the basement stairs. The bare light bulbs hanging down from the ceiling cast a dim glow. I ducked under the first beam.

"Watch your head," I called back to Augie.

The basement ceiling was really, really low. My father once explained to me that the basement had been dug after the house was already built, and they didn't want to go down very far. The floor was made of uneven concrete, rutted and buckling in places, chipped and missing in others to reveal the dirt underneath. The walls were also made of porous concrete, and shelves lined most of the walls. We had to use the shelves to store everything because we couldn't leave anything on the floor. When it rained too hard, the water running into the sewer in front of our house backed up through the drain in the floor and ran into our basement. Then, until it all flowed back out through the drain, our basement was filled with water. Sometime it took a few hours, sometimes a lot longer.

"Just put the snake down over there," I said to Augie.

He put the bag down on the floor.

"We have to build something big enough to hold the snake, but small enough to fit into my room."

"Not to mention strong enough to keep the snake inside. Can you imagine if it got out of the box?" Augie said.

"Let's not even joke about that. Can you get me some wood from over there in the corner?"

"Sure. What do you need?"

"A couple of pieces of two-by-four and one of the big pieces of plywood for starters."

Augie went to get the wood, and I went to get the tools from the workbench. I'd need a hammer, nails and a saw. And of course, some idea of what I was going to build.

Chapter Sixteen

Carefully, trying hard not to disturb the snake inside, I checked the knot on the bag. It was still firm and tight. I wanted to roll the sack over, or pick it up to make sure that there weren't any holes that had been created by the snake pushing against the fibre. But picking it up might wake up the snake. It had been completely still for the past while. And if it was wise to let sleeping dogs lie, it was probably twice as smart not to wake up a sleeping boa constrictor.

I'd been so pleased when the snake finally settled down. It had been unnerving to see the bag moving— especially after Augie had left and I was by myself. He had to get to the synagogue. We'd agreed he'd be back early tomorrow for us to work on our assignment on friendship.

My father came in shortly after Augie left. He hollered down a "hello." It was good just to have some-body else in the house. I guess I could have called him down, asked for his advice and help in finishing up the pen, but I knew he'd be busy doing something—he was always busy doing something—and I didn't want to bother him.

And I was okay, as long as the snake was sleeping . . . it was sleeping, wasn't it? I had a horrible thought. What if it wasn't sleeping? What if it was dead? What if it ran out of air and smothered in the bag? No, it couldn't have. It was a burlap sack, and there were lots and lots of little holes in burlap . . . weren't there?

I put down the hammer. There were still a bunch of small nails I wanted to drive into the joints to secure the walls and screen, but that would have to wait. Slowly, hardly making a sound, I slipped over to the bag. I grabbed it with both hands and lifted it up, feeling the strain in my arms. There was no motion from inside. It felt like dead weight. My stomach did a flip.

"Wake up!" I yelled as I gave the sack a real shake.

Nothing. It either was soundly sleeping . . . or dead. If it was sleeping, I was okay. If it was dead, then I was dead. I couldn't help but think how everybody at school would react—how Frankie would react—if all I had to show for their money was a dead snake. A snake that I'd killed. That would make me as bad as the people who tortured Bogart. Maybe I didn't do it on purpose, but . . . wait. What if it was only a *little* dead! I'd taken first aid in health, and I'd seen hundreds and hundreds of hospital shows on TV. Maybe I could revive it with mouth-to-mouth resuscitation. That thought made me shudder.

Either way, I had to get it out of the bag and into the pen. I started to run upstairs. I needed to get both the snake and the pen into my room. The heavy sack swung like a pendulum as I awkwardly lumbered up the stairs. I staggered into the kitchen. My father was at the kitchen sink, washing the dishes.

"What you got in the bag?" he asked.

"The snake for Mr. Johnston."

"Must be a big snake."

"Pretty big," I said.

"You going to show it to me?" he asked.

"Soon as I put it in the pen," I called back over my shoulder.

"Is that what you were building down in the basement?" he called.

"Yep," I yelled back as I started up the stairs to my room.

I was nowhere near the top of the steps when I heard music flowing down the stairs. My sister was obviously home too. If she saw the bag, she'd ask me what was inside, and if I told her she'd freak. I reached the top of the stairs, and peeked around the corner and down the hall. Her door was closed. Good!

I pushed open the door to my room, stumbled and banged the bag heavily into the door frame. Suddenly the snake came to life and the sack shivered and shook. In shock I almost dropped it. Then my shock gave way to relief. The snake wasn't just alive, it was *very* alive! Thank God!

I put the bag down on the floor. The snake continued to move around. I didn't want to leave it there alone, but I had to go get the pen. I pulled my bedroom door closed. I bounded down the stairs, a few at a time, and then leaped down the final half a dozen, landing with a thunderous thud at the bottom. I scrambled around the corner and through the kitchen.

"Sounded like a truck hit the side of the house," my father said as I ran by.

"No truck . . . just me, sorry," I said as I took to the basement stairs. I had to slow down because these steps were steep and uneven and strangely spaced. I held onto the railing and reached the bottom. I brushed the hammer and nails off the top of the pen. No time for any more nails now. The pen was strong enough. I lifted up the pen and started back up the stairs, struggling to heft it up the steps.

"That's not your finest work," my father said, eyeing the pen.

"It's just for a few days, and then the snake is gone."

"You say that about all the things you bring home," he commented.

"But this time I mean it . . . I mean, I mean it all the time—it's just that this time it's for sure."

My father smiled.

"No, seriously. Like I said, this is for Mr. Johnston and it'll only be here until Monday."

"You must really like this teacher."

"He's a good teacher and we got a real special deal, so we got him a really big snake."

"So you bought a snake on sale?" he asked, laughing out the last few words. It was good to see him laugh— good and rare.

"It's almost six feet long."

"Wow, that is amazing. You have a six-foot snake in your room."

"A little over six feet. Do you want to see it?"

"Definitely," he said, drying his hands on the front of his shirt. "Let me help you with that."

My father took the pen from my hands. He handled it like it was light. I guess for him it was. He followed me up the stairs and into my room.

"The snake is right here in the—" The bag wasn't in the middle of the floor where I'd left it. It couldn't be gone! It had to be right . . . I caught sight of a corner of the bag. It was almost completely under the bed, and it moved as the snake moved within it. I dropped to my knees, grabbed the bag and pulled it out.

"Where do you want me to put this?" my father asked.

"Um, just over here . . . beside my bed." It was practically the only area of floor not already covered with furniture or animal pens. "It's just for two days."

The pen was slightly over three feet long, half as wide and about two feet tall. The top was attached by hinges that allowed the whole thing to open up. A small patch, three inches square, had been cut out of the top and replaced by wire mesh to let in air. I'd put a latch to hold the top in place so the snake couldn't force it open. After all, a boa was nothing more than one large, long, strong muscle.

I opened up the top and placed the bag inside the pen. I fumbled at the knot, and when it came free I rolled the bag back slightly. The snake started to inch its way out. I drew back my hand.

"That is some snake," my father said, obviously impressed, as the snake kept flowing from the bag. As it stretched out, its head reached the farthest corner of the pen while most of it remained inside the sack. It started up the side of the pen and looked like it was trying to get away. Instinctively I reached out to grab it and pull it back. Like a bolt of lightning, the snake swung its head around and lunged at me. I dropped the snake and slammed down the lid. Almost in the same motion I snapped the latch closed, locking the lid in place.

"That snake can really move," my father noted.

"Snake! What snake?"

I turned around. My sister Janice was standing at my bedroom door.

"You have a snake!" she screeched. "You know I hate

snakes! I shouldn't have to live in the same house with a snake! Isn't it bad enough that I have to live with all those other awful animals?"

"Janice—"

"I hate snakes! I refuse to stay in the same house with a snake!" she screamed.

"Janice, it's—"

"They're so slimy and awful and they make my skin crawl!"

"Janice, it's going—"

"And I don't care if it is in your room. Just knowing it's in the same house as me is more than I can stand! It has to go!"

"Janice, it's going to go," I finally managed to blurt out when she stopped to take a breath.

"It is?" she asked, sounding surprised.

I think my answer caught her off guard. She was expecting a fight. "It'll be gone by Monday morning."

"Monday?"

"I'll be bringing it to school."

"For a while or forever?" she asked suspiciously.

"Forever. We're giving it to my science teacher, Mr. Johnston."

"What do you mean *we*?" she asked.

"Me and Augie, but I guess really everybody in the whole school is part of it. Almost every kid contributed money to buy the snake."

She looked at me and then at the pen by my feet.

"How big is it?" Her face was calm and quiet. Much calmer and quieter than I knew she must be feeling inside.

"It's not that big ... for a boa constrictor," I answered.

"Oh my God," she muttered as she backed away a couple of steps.

"It's not big enough to hurt you," I said reassuringly.

"How big is it?" she asked again.

"About six feet long."

She gasped.

"And it's like I said, it isn't big enough to hurt you."

"But it could hurt something smaller, couldn't it?"

"Sure . . . of course."

"Like my cat or even Candy," she said.

"I don't know about Candy. She can probably take care of herself."

"But it could hurt my Gandalf!" She turned directly to Dad. "This isn't fair. You have to make him get that killer out of our house immediately! Isn't it bad enough that my poor Gandalf has to put up with those ugly alley cats of his when he goes outside! Now my cat isn't even safe in the house!"

"Your cat is safe as long as he stays out of my room. Which reminds me, I want him to stay out of my room *forever*. I want him to stop using Ollie's pen as a litter box."

My sister chuckled. She always found it amusing that her cat did that in my room.

"I'm glad you think it's funny now, but just wait. Ollie's getting bigger all the time. It's just a matter of time before Gandalf becomes alligator chow. Maybe you better save some of your money to buy a little kitty walker, 'cause I'm positive Ollie could take off a foot."

That wiped the smirk off her face. "Well, that's it, then. Both the snake *and* that alligator have to leave immediately!"

"Ollie's not going anywhere—and just where do you think I can bring the snake to?" I demanded.

"I don't know and I don't care! I just know that I refuse to sleep in the same house as that evil serpent!"

"Good, then, maybe you can go and stay someplace else!"

"Maybe I will and—"

"Both of you stop it!" my father said.

"But, Dad, it's just—"

"Now!" he snapped. "The alligator stays and the snake is going to leave the house—"

"But, Dad, I can't just—"

"On Monday," he continued. "And it would be wise if the door to your room stayed closed. Not just now, but always, so the cat stays away from the alligator."

"But I don't like to sleep with the door closed."

"You're just going to have to learn to like it," he said. "Any arguments?"

When my father said "any arguments," it meant, don't even *try* to argue.

"Okay . . . sure," I answered.

"Good. Now I want you to take the snake out of the pen and show it to your sister," he said.

"I don't want to see it!" she screamed, backing right out of my room until she was standing in the hall. Finally she and I could agree on something about the snake—I didn't want to show it to her any more than she wanted to see it.

"It's better to confront your fears than to run from them," my father said calmly. He turned to me. "Show her there's nothing to be afraid of. Pick it up."

I'd originally thought he just wanted me to open the pen. This was worse. I didn't want to admit it, but I was feeling nervous—no, worse than nervous. I was scared. But there was no way I could show it. If they saw how I felt, I might have to take the snake someplace else right now. Besides, my father was here. Nothing could happen with him around.

My father and sister were both staring at me. Waiting. Maybe it wasn't just my sister who needed to confront her fears. And it wasn't like I didn't know what I was doing. I'd picked up Bogart dozens and dozens of times.

But this wasn't Bogart.

Quickly, before I had time to rethink it, I reached down and clicked the latch, unlocking the lid. I raised my hands and readied myself.

"Could you open up the top so I can grab the snake?" I asked my father.

He opened the lid, and almost instantly the boa's head started to climb the side. I reached out with my left hand and grabbed it just behind the head. It was so thick I couldn't close my hand around it. It reacted to my touch and threw its coils, trying to wrap itself around my arm. I knew exactly what I had to do next. I reached out, and with the other hand, I took hold of it just by the tail. I had him!

Straining under the weight of the snake, I lifted him up and out of the cage. As I turned toward my sister, I could see a look of pure disgust on her face. That look alone was almost worth having to hold the snake. It was heavy, though, and I knew I couldn't hold it out that way for long. I lifted it over my head and slung it over my shoulders. That was the way I'd always held Bogart.

"That's disgusting!" Janice shrieked.

"Actually, it's a pretty snake," my father said. "Nice browns and blacks in an interesting pattern." He reached out and stroked it. "It feels very smooth and warm. Do you want to touch it?" he asked my sister.

"Not in a million years!" she yelled and rushed off. I heard the door to her bedroom slam shut.

"I guess that means no," I said.

My father looked amused. "I guess so. You'd better put it away now."

"Sure . . . no problem."

The words were hardly out of my mouth when the snake bucked and twisted and I lost my grip on its tail. As I struggled to regain my hold, the snake tried to coil around me.

"Could you please help me grab ahold of—" I stopped mid-sentence as I secured my hold, and then in one motion flipped the boa off my shoulders so I was holding it in front of me. I placed it in the pen, and before it could react, I let go and closed the lid.

"Good," my father said. "I'm glad it's back in the pen."

His voice sounded different. I glanced at him and saw the strangest look in his eyes.

"You don't like snakes, do you," I asked.

"It's a lot more than not liking them. They scare me."

"You? You're scared of snakes?" I asked. I was shocked. I'd never even imagined that my father was afraid of *anything*.

"Have been since I was a little kid," he answered.

"But why did you come up here to see it . . . or make me take it out of the box? You even *touched* it." That didn't make any sense to me.

"I had to," he said, and then paused. "It wasn't just

Janice I was talking to when I said you have to confront your fears. That's something we all have to work on. Understand?"

"I think so," I mumbled.

"Good. Now click the latch to lock the snake in. And I want you to pile something heavy, like some of the encyclopedias, on top of the lid. Just in case."

That sounded like a fine idea to me, as well. Somehow I felt less safe knowing my father had been scared.

I rearranged my pillow for the three hundredth time and shuffled my feet around inside my sleeping bag. I hadn't been able to get to sleep. No big surprise there. There was always something to worry about. At least tonight I *knew* what I was worried about. I turned over and faced the pen. There, close enough for me to reach out and touch it, was the snake. In the dark I could see the outline of the wooden structure, the books piled on top. The whole set of encyclopedias. I wasn't taking any chances.

A couple of times I thought I could hear the boa moving around inside. Likely it was just the sound of another one of my animals. The night was always filled with the sounds of somebody moving around in a cage, or eating or squawking, or drinking or running around in an exercise wheel.

I was tempted to get up and peer through the little mesh window on the top of the pen. I knew there wasn't any point, though. The room was dark and the pen was darker. Even if I looked I wouldn't be able to see anything.

I knew the snake was in there. I knew the latch was in place and the books were on top. I knew it couldn't get out. And I also knew that I was going to get even less sleep tonight than usual.

Chapter Seventeen

"So, what's this assignment all about?" Augie asked.

"What?" My mind had been elsewhere, and it took a split second before my brain caught up to my mouth.

"Assignment . . . the thing we're here to do instead of being out on the street playing hockey."

"It's on friendship. I've told you that. Didn't you even read the sheet?" I asked.

"I didn't see any point in reading it," Augie said. "I knew you would have read it more carefully than I ever could, and then you'd explain it to me." Augie paused. "You look beat."

"Gee, thanks."

"Like you didn't get any sleep last night."

"I slept . . . a little," I admitted.

"Did the snake creep you out?"

"No, of course . . . well . . . a little, I guess."

"I don't think I would have slept at all if it was in my room," Augie said.

He walked across my room and bent to peer through the little mesh window of the snake's pen. He moved his head around, trying to see inside. Why couldn't he see it? It was a big snake . . . had it gotten out or—

"It's all curled up in a ball in the corner," Augie said, and I breathed a big sigh of relief.

"So, are you going to tell me about the assignment or what?" Augie asked.

"I've already told you about it. It's about friendship. There's a whole lot of questions we have to answer about our friendship. It's like a questionnaire."

"That sounds easy."

"We'll see."

Augie took the assignment from my hands. "We'll work as a team. I'll do all the writing and you do most of the thinking."

"Sounds reasonable," I said.

Augie looked down at the paper. "This first question is easy. How long have you been friends?"

"That is easy. Just over three years."

"Yep, since the first day of grade five . . . which answers question number two. Where did you meet?"

"In the hall outside room twenty-three at General Mercer Public School."

Augie nodded and I could see him write one word, *school*, on the line.

"Question three. What things do you and your friend do together?"

"Sports, for one thing," I said.

"And going places like the museum, and the Canadian National Exhibition, and downtown."

"And helping each other with school," I added.

"And let's not forget talking about girls."

"Don't you mean you *talking* and me *listening*?" I suggested.

"I guess so, but it is a shared activity."

I had the urge to lean over and look at what Augie had written, but I knew he wouldn't appreciate me checking on him. He put down the pen and started to read the next question.

"I don't get this one," he said. "Friendship is often based on commonality. List all the things you two have in common." He looked up at me. "What exactly does that mean?"

"That one is tricky. I've been thinking about it."

"Good. So what do I write?"

"I don't know," I said, shaking my head.

"What do you mean, you don't know? Don't you understand the question either?"

"I understand the question," I said. "I just don't have an answer."

Augie looked surprised by my answer, or I guess my lack of answer.

"Then, tell you what, you explain the question to me, and I'll try to figure out the answer," Augie said.

"Sure. The question is asking us to list all the things

we have in common, the things about us that are the same, that we share."

"You had me worried for a second. That's easy too," Augie said confidently.

"Well . . . what exactly do we have in common?" I asked.

"For starters, we're both . . . um, extremely handsome."

"Yeah, right. Seriously."

"Okay, then, maybe we both have the same . . . you and me both . . ." He looked perplexed.

"That's as far as I got too," I said.

"Come on, we have to have other things in common."

I shook my head. "Think about it. I'm twelve and you're fourteen. You live above a store and I live in a house. I have pets and you don't. Your father owns a business and my father works in a warehouse. You're Jewish and I'm not. I have an older sister and you have an older brother. You have blond hair and I have brown hair."

"Even our families," Augie said. "I live with both parents and you live with just your father because your mother . . ." He let the sentence trail off. He knew I didn't like to talk about this stuff.

"We both have blue eyes," Augie said, changing the subject.

"I don't think that a friendship can be based on eye colour," I said.

"Come on, we have to have other things in common."

"Not that I can think of. Even school. It's easy for me. I'm smart in school and—"

"And I'm stupid," Augie finished.

"That wasn't what I was going to say!" I protested. "I was going to say that I'm smart in school and you're smart in life."

"What do you mean?" Augie asked.

"You have to be one of the smartest people I know. It's just that it doesn't always come out at school."

"Doesn't always?" he questioned. "How about hardly never?"

"Don't say that," I said.

He shrugged. "Well, if I'm so smart, how come I can't figure out the answer to this question?"

"I'm smart and I can't figure it out either. We just don't seem to have much in common."

"But we're friends. Best friends. Maybe it isn't us that's wrong. Maybe the *question* is wrong."

"What do you mean?" I asked.

"Maybe friendship isn't based on having things in common. Have you ever heard that expression 'opposites attract'?"

"Sure. Like on a magnet. Put two positive sides

together and they push each other apart, but opposite charges attract."

"Well, maybe that's us. Opposites attract. We'll just write down that the question is wrong!" Augie said, and he started to write.

I didn't know if that was such a great idea if we wanted to get good marks, but for once I didn't care. Augie wrote down some words, ended the sentence with an exclamation mark and then underlined it all . . . twice.

"And now the final question. Is there something about your friend that you don't know or don't understand? And if so, what?" He looked up at me. "Well?"

"I can't think of anything. I think I know you pretty well," I said. "And you?"

"Naw. I think I know you pretty good. I understand almost everything about you."

"What do you mean 'almost everything'? Is there something you want to know?" I asked.

He paused, and I knew by the look on his face that there was something.

"It's not important," he said.

"What is it?" I asked.

"Well, I was just wondering . . . about your mother . . ."

"You know about my mother," I snapped.

"Of course I know about her. I was just wondering, you know, why you never tell anybody else about her."

"What do you mean?" I demanded.

"This is hard to explain," he said. "And I don't want to hurt your feelings or get you mad or anything."

It was already too late for that.

"It's like with Elyse and her mother, and with other people. When they mention your mother, or ask a question, you either don't answer, or sort of say something that would make them think she was still alive."

"I don't have to tell everybody about my private life!" I protested. "And besides, I don't even think I do that."

"You do," Augie said softly.

"I do not!"

"You even did it with me when we first met."

I didn't know what to say.

"The first time I came here I asked if your mother was home, and you said, 'She's not here right now.' Do you remember saying that?"

I shook my head. I didn't remember, but it sounded like something I would have said.

I felt my tongue start to shake—the first sign that maybe I was going to cry—and I bit down on the inside of my mouth. The little shot of pain drove the tears away.

"I know it must be hard," Augie said. "Having your mother die."

I bit down harder.

"And it must be scary, you know, it just being you

and your sister and father. Where's the rest of your family?"

"Around," I said quietly. "I have some aunts and uncles and cousins."

"What about grandparents? If something happened to my mother, her mother would practically live at my house!"

I felt like I'd had the air in my lungs removed. "My grandmother—she did live here."

"She did?" Augie asked.

I nodded my head. "She and my grandfather."

"When?"

"From before I was born."

"When did they move out?"

I walked to the window and looked out. I fought the urge to just say 'yes' they moved out. "They . . . died. One and then the other—within a year of my mother going."

"I had no idea," he said. "I'm sorry. I guess I shouldn't have asked."

"That's okay," I said, biting down on my cheek so hard I could taste blood.

Augie put a hand on my shoulder. "You know what? I just thought of something else we have in common.

"You have?" I asked.

"Yes. We both have an older brother."

"I don't have an older brother."

"Yes, you do . . . me," Augie said pointing at himself. "And we also have other things in common. We both take care of each other, just in different ways. And you know what else we have in common? Neither of us would ever hurt the other one, at least not on purpose, right?"

I nodded. I knew what he meant. He knew how hard this had been for me and he was saying that he wasn't trying to hurt my feelings.

"Good, so let's finish writing this sucker up so we can stop working and just enjoy ourselves. Okay?"

"Yeah, that would be good," I said quietly.

"And then we can get ready for tomorrow. What are you going to wear?" Augie asked.

"I hadn't really thought about it. I guess what I'm wearing now."

"I was thinking that maybe we could have one more thing in common. What do you think about my pants?"

"They're . . . nice."

"They're also new."

"No they're not. You've had those pants for a long time," I said.

"Nope. I've had another pair of pants just like them, except smaller, too small . . . about your size. Do you want to try them on?"

"I don't know . . ."

"Come on, if you wore them we'd have another thing in common. Okay?"

I shrugged. "I guess I could."

"Let me write down the answer to the last question

and then we'll go over to my place, grab some lunch, you check out the pants, and then we'll go and play some hockey."

"I don't know if I should leave the snake alone," I said.

"Get somebody else to watch it. Maybe your sister."

I laughed. "Right, like that's going to happen! She slept at one of her friend's places last night, and she's going to do the same thing tonight, to get away from the snake."

"Ask your father to just check on it every now and again. It's not like it's going to get out."

"I don't know."

"Come on," Augie pleaded. "It'll be okay. And besides, my mother was cooking soup when I left. Your favourite . . . chicken noodle."

He was right. It was my favourite. I could practically smell it. "Okay, for a little while."

"Hold still or I'm going to stick you with one of these pins," Augie's mother said through closed lips, which were holding more pins.

I was standing on a chair in the back of the Levy's store. She was working on altering Augie's old pants so that they would fit me. Despite the fact that they were too small for Augie, they were still too big for me.

"Quit fidgeting," she said.

"I'm trying."

I was feeling nervous. First, I didn't feel right about taking something for nothing—it felt like charity. And now I felt even worse with Augie's mother fussing over me and—

"Ow!" I howled, jumping as a pin stuck into my leg.

"Stand still!" she demanded. "What do you have, ants in your pants?"

"I'll try to stay stiller . . . I promise."

"Good!"

She worked away at the bottom of the left leg, pinning it up to the right length.

From my perch on the chair I could see the entire store and right out the front window to the people and cars and streetcars passing by on Rogers Road. There were a few customers in the store, and both Augie and his father were helping them.

"There, finished with that," Mrs. Levy said.

I went to climb off the chair, and she stopped me.

"Where do you think you're going, young man?" she asked.

"I was getting down. You said you were finished."

"I am finished. Finished with the legs. Now I have to adjust the waist." She took hold of the waistband and pulled it out and away from my waist.

"You're too skinny!" she said loudly. "You need to eat more!"

"I had three bowls of soup at lunch," I protested.

"I don't mean just now. I mean every day. Don't I always tell you to eat more every single time you eat with us?"

"Always."

There was no doubt about that statement. She was always trying to get me to eat. When I was sharing a meal with the Levys, she'd pile my plate high, and then add more food before I'd even come close to finishing what she'd put there in the first place. Augie said it was almost impossible at his house to ever clear the food off your plate. And she was always telling me I was too skinny.

"To be healthy you have to have more meat on your bones. Do you want to get sick?" she demanded. "If you lived here for a few weeks and ate with us, I wouldn't need to be taking these pants in."

"Maybe not," I agreed. "But you might have to be letting them out."

She laughed. It was a nice laugh.

Of course, it wasn't just that I ate well when I was at the Levys', but that I ate differently. They ate all sorts of things that my father never made for us. Things like latkes, and corned beef, and bagels and lox, and borscht. I'd never heard of any of them before I came here to eat, but I tried them and liked them a lot.

"So do you still want to be a dog doctor?" she asked as she started to tack the waist in place.

"Yep, I'd like to be a veterinarian."

"Why not a people doctor? You'd make good money, you'd be respected by the members of your community, and what mother . . . or father wouldn't want to say, my son the *doctor*." She paused and looked up at me. "There, now I'm finished everything. You go into the change room and get back into your other pants."

I carefully climbed off the chair, trying hard not to get stuck by any of the dozens of pins tacking my pants into place. I slipped into the change room and slowly and deliberately took off the pants, making sure not only that I didn't get pricked again, but that I didn't dislodge any of the pins.

I caught sight of myself in the full-length mirror covering one of the walls of the change room. My hair was standing straight at the top. I'd try to remember to take a bath and have a shampoo tonight. It had been a while since I'd done either.

I couldn't help but also notice my legs reflected back at me. They *were* on the thin side. I guess all of me was.

Not that I'd ever live anywhere except with my father, but I wondered what it would be like to live with Augie's family for a couple of weeks. I was sure I would put on weight. And I did like Augie's family, especially his mother. Augie complained about how she was always "nagging" him about things. What to eat, where he was going, who he was going to be with, what time he went to bed at night, what he was going to wear. Personally I thought that wouldn't be so bad.

My father was always so busy that he didn't have time to nag me. I guess it would have been different if my mother was around. I guess. I really couldn't remember very much about her. And sometimes I thought that the things I remembered were what I'd been told, rather than what I recalled. The only clear memory I had was when I was about four. I was sitting in a wheelbarrow and my mother was pushing me and we were both laughing. I probably laughed a lot back then.

I'd been told by people that she was nice. But then again, what else would people say? It isn't like they'd say bad things about a dead lady to her son.

I closed my eyes and tried to picture her in my mind. The image was there, but it seemed blurry. Maybe when I got home—if my father wasn't right there—I could go into the big cedar chest and pull out some pictures of her. Janice told me that Dad put them all away the day after she died. I was too little to remember any of that either. I just remember the pictures always being there in the chest.

"Pass the pants over to me!" Mrs. Levy called through the door, startling me out of my thoughts.

"Yeah, sure," I said as I picked them up off the floor and then handed them over the top of the change room door.

"I'll have them sewn up in a few minutes," she said as the pants disappeared.

I quickly grabbed my pants and pulled them on. I zipped up the fly and snapped the top button into place. I slipped my feet into my shoes and bent down to do up the laces.

"Hey, Ricky!" Augie called out. "My mom wants to know if you want to stay for supper."

I opened up the door to face him. "Not tonight. It's Sunday, so my father was cooking today."

"Stew?" he asked.

"Probably," I answered, although there was no doubt about it. Stew was about all my father made, except for boiled potatoes. And actually, he put boiled potatoes in the stew too.

"Don't you ever get tired of stew?"

"We don't eat it all the time."

"Well, how about eating it one less time. Eat with us tonight."

"I can't," I said.

"Of course you can. Your father never says no."

"He does, sometimes." I hoped Augie didn't ask me when, so I wouldn't have to make up any more lies. My dad basically let me do anything I wanted.

"It's just that I don't want to leave the snake alone any longer," I said.

"Call your father. He'd go upstairs and check it again if you asked, wouldn't he?"

"He would, but I also want to finish up my home-work."

"Come on, I've never known you to wait until Sunday evening to finish your homework."

"It's just reading. I want to finish a book I'm reading. And besides, I want to get ready for tomorrow."

"Get ready how?" Augie asked.

"I figure we have to say something when we give Mr. Johnston the snake."

"I was thinking we could say something like, 'Here's your snake,' and then we hand it to him," Augie joked.

"I was hoping for something a little better than that."

"Leave it to me and I'll figure out what we should say," Augie said.

I knew I could trust him to come up with something good. "But I also want to get *me* ready."

"What are you going to do?" Augie asked.

"You know, take a bath, shampoo my hair . . . just get ready."

"Good plan. We're going to be standing in front of the whole school so we should look as good as we can. Do you know what shirt you're going to wear with your new pants?"

"I'm not sure. Something different from what you're going to wear. We're already going to look too cute with the matching pants."

"We're just going to look good. So are you going to stay for supper?"

I shook my head. "I want to eat with my father. He'll be by himself if I'm not there."

"Okay, then, I'll be there tomorrow . . . early. Do you think you can be ready on time, just once?"

"No problem. I figure I'll be up early . . . really early."

Chapter Eighteen

I opened my eyes. It was light, so it was morning. I wondered how early it was. I rolled over and looked at the clock. Almost eight o'clock! I should have been up an hour ago! I practically jumped out of bed. Augie would be here in just a few minutes. How could I sleep that long? I remembered my father yelling up to me when he left at six-thirty to tell me he was heading to work, and I just closed my eyes for a second. Or so I thought.

I ran to the bathroom, grabbed my toothbrush and squeezed out some paste. Normally I'd wait until after breakfast to brush my teeth, but I knew I didn't have time to eat anything.

I charged back into my room. The pants, a clean shirt—one with a collar so it would look fancy—socks and boxers were laid out on the chair by my desk. I had kicked off my p.j. pants and started to put on my boxers, when I heard pounding on the front door. It had to be Augie.

"I'm coming!" I yelled. I pulled on the pants and did them up.

Candy was going crazy down there. I could hear her scratching at the door, trying to get through the wood at

Augie on the outside. I grabbed my shirt off the back of the chair and threw it over my head as I ran for the stairs.

"I'll be right there!" I called, as the knocking came again. "Keep your shirt on!"

Candy looked like she was trying to dig right through the door. I took hold of her collar and dragged her away. I'd hauled her no more than a dozen feet, when to my complete surprise, the front door opened and Augie popped in. He never came in until I had Candy safely locked away.

"Hurry up!" he called out.

Candy dug in her feet and started to snap and snarl as she strained to get back to the door and Augie. I tightened my grip on her collar and hauled her away, almost throwing her into the living room. I slammed the door shut behind her, locking her away.

"Come on, let's go!" Augie said. "We don't want to get there too late."

"We still have plenty of time," I said. Maybe not enough time to eat anything, but certainly enough time to get to school.

"We have to arrive early. We don't want everybody in the schoolyard to be bugging us to see the snake. What if Mr. Johnston is on yard duty and comes over to see what everybody is looking at? That would be the end of the surprise."

"I hadn't thought of that. I can be ready in five minutes."

"Let's make it ten, so you'll have time to do something with your hair," Augie said.

"My hair? What's wrong with my hair? I washed it last night."

"Just before you went to bed, right?"

"Yeah . . . how did you know that?" I asked.

"Go and have a look at yourself in the mirror."

There was only one mirror in the whole house. It was in the bathroom, above the sink. I sprinted up the stairs and into the bathroom. I recoiled from my reflection. My hair was sticking out in all directions. I looked like a young Albert Einstein.

"Don't worry, we can fix it," Augie said. He was standing in the doorway of the bathroom. "Just soak it down with water. That'll flatten it out. And then you can comb it."

"Sure . . . can you get the snake while I'm fixing my hair?"

"By myself?" Augie asked. He sounded shocked and unsure.

"Don't worry he won't . . ." I didn't finish. It didn't make sense to accuse him of being scared of the snake when that's how I felt myself. I hadn't taken it out of the pen since my father had insisted that I show it to my sister on Saturday.

"Just hang on a minute, then," I said.

I turned on the tap of the bathtub and plunged my head beneath the stream of cold water. In one quick motion I'd not only soaked my head, but washed my face, and also made certain that I was really, really awake. I turned off the tap, grabbed a towel and started to dry my face and hair.

"What are we going to carry the snake in?" Augie asked.

"I just thought we'd use the burlap sack again."

"That'll work fine . . . once we get it *in* the bag."

Instantly I thought back to the first time it went into the bag at Reptile World. Could we do it with just two people? But, what choice did we have? Unless we just left it in the pen and carried the pen to . . . that was stupid. There was no way we could carry something that heavy, that far. The snake *had* to go into the bag.

"We can do it, don't worry," I said, trying my best to sound confident. I wasn't sure if I was trying to convince Augie, or me.

I pulled the shirt back over my head and hurried into my room. Augie followed.

"Can you take all the books off the top while I get on my socks and shoes?"

"That I can do by myself," Augie said.

I sat down on the edge of my bed and started to pull on my socks, while Augie began to remove the books.

"Have you figured out what you're going to say when we give Mr. Johnston the snake?" I asked.

"First off, *you're* going to hand him the snake," Augie corrected me. "And second, I do know."

"Well . . ."

"I'm just going to say how sad everybody was about what happened to Bogart, and because he's such a wonderful teacher, that everybody in the school chipped in to buy him a new snake."

"Sounds good," I said as I started to tie up my shoes.

"And I'm going to say how this whole thing was your idea," Augie said.

"But we did it together!" I protested. "You, Elyse and me."

"Elyse and I talked. She says she just helped a little and doesn't think she deserves any credit. Besides, it was your idea."

"But I couldn't have done it without you."

"Maybe, maybe not," Augie said. "But it was your idea, and I think you deserve the credit."

"But—"

"But nothing!" Augie said, holding up his hands. "That's what I'm going to say, and if you don't like it, then *you* can make the speech *and* hold the snake!"

That was so like Augie. He was a good guy. I wished I'd put that down on the assignment about friendship.

I finished tying up my second shoelace and looked up at Augie. He was standing there, holding a book in each hand, a stricken look on his face.

"Ricky . . . is the screen on the top of the pen supposed to be bent up like that?"

The little square of wire mesh was pushed up and

away from the pen. It looked like it had come away from two of the sides.

I suddenly felt like somebody had punched me in the stomach, and my head started to spin.

"It shouldn't be like that . . . should it?" Augie asked again.

I shook my head ever so slightly. I didn't want to let my mind go to the next step. The snake couldn't have gotten out through that little hole, could it?

"Ricky, say something," Augie pleaded.

He was obviously thinking what I didn't dare say.

"Open the lid," I croaked, my voice sounding strange to my ears.

Augie didn't move.

"Open it!" I ordered.

Augie shifted around to the back of the pen while I moved right in front of it. I positioned myself to be ready to pounce on the snake. I hoped, and prayed, it would pop out the instant Augie opened the lid.

Augie grabbed the lid with both hands and tried to pull it open. "It's stuck!" he yelled. "I can't open it!"

"Hold on, I have to undo the latch!"

I clicked it open, and at the same instant, Augie pulled again and the lid crashed open. I jumped forward and . . . the box was empty.

Chapter Nineteen

"Oh my God," Augie said softly. "Could it really get out through that little hole?"

I stepped forward, almost climbing right into the box, and thrust my arm through the mesh. It pushed aside and my arm sank through the mesh up to my elbow. I needed proof—to see with my own eyes what I already knew.

"It's gone!" Augie exclaimed. "Gone!"

"No, no . . . it isn't," I said, shaking my head.

"Of course it is!" Augie said, sounding hysterical. "Can't you see it isn't in the box! It's gone!"

"I know it isn't in the box!" I bellowed back. "I'm not blind! I just mean it isn't gone. It's here . . . somewhere in my bedroom."

"In here?" Augie said, looking around. He looked like that thought unnerved him more than the fact that the snake was gone.

I nodded. "We have to search for it."

"We . . . us . . . you and me?"

"Who else?" I asked.

"How about your father?" Augie asked.

"He's on his way to work right now. But even if I could reach him, he couldn't leave work to help us."

"Then, your sister. Has she left for work yet?"

"Remember, she's been sleeping at her friend's place the past two nights. Anyway, if she knew the snake was loose somewhere in the house, she'd run out the front door screaming at the top of her lungs."

"There has to be somebody who can help us," Augie snapped. "There has to be!"

"Like who? What do you think we can do, call the police or fire department or ambulance?"

"No, of course not, but there has to be somebody. How about Reptile World!"

"They're not even open yet, and even if they were, do you think they'd send somebody halfway across the city to help us? It's just you and me. We have to find it."

"But where?"

"Here, in my bedroom. It has to be here. It was in the pen when I went to bed last night, and my door was closed all night, so it has to be in my room," I reasoned. Thank goodness my father had made me close my door the past two nights.

"It could be somewhere else," Augie said. "Your door was open when I followed you upstairs. It could have got out then."

"It couldn't have!" I insisted. "I was just downstairs for a few seconds, and we would have seen it if it tried to go downstairs."

"But what about another room up here?" Augie asked.

I took a few quick steps out to the doorway of my bedroom and peered down the hall. My father's door was open but my sister's was closed. If the boa had got out, at least it hadn't got in her room. I stepped back into my room and closed the door, sealing me, Augie and the snake in . . . I hoped.

"We'll start here in my room."

"And if we don't find it?"

"We'll look in my father's room."

"And if we don't find it there?"

"We'll search the rest of the house," I said.

"And if we don't find it there? If we just plain don't find it?"

"We have to find it. I can just imagine what my father will say, and my sister, too, if we don't. She'll kill me!"

"That's not the biggest problem," Augie said.

"What do you mean?"

"I'm thinking about what's going to happen at school."

"I still don't understand," I said.

"You . . . me . . . we . . . we've taken money from hundreds of kids to buy a snake for Mr. Johnston. If we don't show up with a snake, or their money, *they're* going to kill us."

"I . . . I hadn't thought of that. Maybe they'll understand."

"I'm sure some of them will understand," Augie said. "And others will just understand that they want to get in line to take turns kicking our butts."

I swallowed hard. I thought about what Frankie had said to me. I could picture him and a couple of his friends letting us know exactly how they felt about things. "Maybe we better start looking."

There was a large pile of stuff on the floor in the centre of my room. Everything had been taken out of my closet and dumped. Drawers had been opened and emptied, the contents added to the growing pile. Pens and cages had been moved away from the walls so nothing could hide behind them. Each time I moved a cage I checked it carefully. I wanted to make sure that the latch was in place, sealing the animals in safely. I didn't want the boa to be feeding on any of my pets. To a boa, they were just food.

"Well, that's it, we're officially late," Augie said, pointing to the clock on my wall.

We'd agreed it was better to arrive late *with* the snake than on time without it. Actually, I'd pretty well decided that if we couldn't find the snake I was never going to school again.

"I've got to use the phone," Augie said as he left my room and started down the stairs.

"Who are you going to call?" I yelled out.

"The school."

"The school? Why are you calling the school?" He didn't answer me. Maybe he hadn't heard my question. I slammed my bedroom door behind me and hurried down the stairs after him.

"Why are you calling—"

Augie put a finger to his lips to silence me. He was holding the phone.

"Hello, is this the office person you call about children being late?" Augie asked with an accent—it was his father's accent and voice!

"My boy Augie will not be in this morning. He's home taking care of some snake," Augie said.

There was silence while he listened to the response on the other end.

"Yes, it is nice of him and that Ricky boy to raise the money. Nice boys is what they are. Honest, too, and smart!"

Again Augie listened to a reply I couldn't hear.

"That's so nice of you," he said, continuing to sound like his father. "And you sound like a nice lady. Where do you do your clothes shopping? You should drop by my store, it's on Rogers Road. You come by and I'll give you a deal . . . ten percent, no, make that fifteen percent off the list price. I'll give you such a deal!"

Augie grinned broadly as he waited for her reply.

"Oh, and I forget to mention. His friend, Ricky—his papa asked me to tell you that his son would be late, as well. The two of them are here with me in the back of the store."

Augie nodded.

"Yes, I know his father should have called, but you know, he's a single parent, it's hard for him to do everything. The boys will be there in time for the assembly. I may even come in myself . . . and remember, come by the store and I'll give you such a deal! Goodbye."

Augie deposited the phone back in the cradle.

"There, that gives us a little time. Let's get back to looking."

We rushed back upstairs to my room.

"I don't even think it's in here," Augie said.

"We haven't looked every place. Help me move the bookshelf so we can look behind it."

Augie and I muscled it away from the wall, a few books dropping as the shelf skidded across the floor. I looked behind it. Nothing but dust.

"Do you think it could be in there?" Augie said, pointing to Ollie's large pen. Do snakes burrow down in sand?"

"I'm not sure. Maybe."

I came forward until I was standing beside Augie, looking down in the sand.

"I don't see anything. At least, on the surface."

I looked over at Ollie. He was in the water, only his

eyes above the waterline, staring at me. I didn't like the way he was looking back at me.

"Maybe if you dig into the sand, it's just below the surface," Augie suggested.

I needed something to move aside the sand. I reached out to the pile in the centre of the floor and grabbed a coat hanger. With the end of it, I started to probe the sand. I began at the end farthest away from the water— and Ollie—and moved in that direction.

It was funny, but I had mixed feelings about the snake being in there. Obviously I wanted to find the snake, but I almost hoped it wouldn't "jump" out at me.

"It's not in here," I said with a sigh of both relief and disappointment.

"Actually, I didn't think it would be," Augie said.

"You didn't?" Why had he suggested it, then?

"I just figured that if it had gotten into the alligator pen, it would have eaten Ollie."

He had a point there. A six-foot boa could eat an alligator the size of Ollie.

"So I guess it isn't in your room. Where do we search next?"

"We'll start up here in my father's room. If we don't find it there, we go to the main floor. And if we have no luck there, we'll go into the basement."

"That'll take forever," Augie said.

"It better not. We have to find it before my father and sister get home tonight."

"Really we have to find it before one o'clock. I only got us excused from school until then. If we don't show by then, we have to call the school and make some sort of excuse. If not, everybody will be going to the gym for the assembly."

My stomach did a flip. I could just imagine everybody in there, sitting, squirming, talking, laughing and waiting. Waiting for us to go up on stage with the snake. And then, not showing up.

"Listen, we don't have time to look everywhere. We have to think this through," Augie said. "Let's just sit down for a minute."

"We don't have time to sit down!" I protested.

"The way I see it, we don't have time *not* to think it through. Tell me about boa constrictors. I need more information so I can figure out where it went."

"I don't have time to give you a science lesson, Augie, we have to look for the snake!"

"I'm not talking a science lesson, I'm talking about some basic facts." Augie pulled out the chair from my desk and sat down. "Now, boas like to climb, right?"

"Yeah, of course. They hang out in trees."

"Good, that's one piece of information. We should make sure to look high before we look low. They also can get through very small spaces, judging by the size of the hole he escaped through."

"He could get through a hole even smaller than that," I said.

"More good information. Now, how long can it go without food and water?" Augie asked.

"It had just eaten when we picked it up on Saturday, so it can go a week or two or even three without eating," I explained.

"And drinking?"

"I'm not really sure, but I think only a few days at most."

"Good, then that might be the secret to catching it," Augie said. "Maybe what we have to do is build some sort of snake trap—you're good with wood and tools—baited with pans of water. We'll put them in different parts of the house and then wait for the snake to come out."

"That could take days! We don't have days . . . we don't even have hours!" I moaned.

"Okay, so that won't help us today, but it will help us eventually, if nothing else works," Augie said. He suddenly stood up and walked over to the snake's pen. He then climbed inside and stood in the middle of the box.

"What are you doing?" I demanded.

"Thinking like a snake. I just need more information."

"More information?"

"Yeah, how do you expect me to think like a snake if I don't know enough about them? Tell me all you know about boa constrictors, just anything you can think of."

"This is crazy!" I exclaimed.

"Maybe. Just tell me things."

There was no point in arguing. I didn't have a better idea. "Um . . . they're reptiles. They are carnivores so they eat only meat." This was stupid.

Augie was standing in the pen with his eyes closed. "Go on," he said. "Give me more!"

"Um . . . they . . . um, have hinged jaws so they can eat things much bigger than them. Like all reptiles they're cold-blooded. They come from South America . . . they live in jungles . . ."

"Hot places. They like hot places."

"Sure, all reptiles like hot places. They like to sit on a stone or log and bask in the sun and—"

"Shh!" Augie hissed at me.

I wasn't sure if he wanted me to be quiet or he was doing a snake impression because he was thinking like a snake.

As I watched silently, Augie opened his eyes and then stepped out of the pen. He took a step forward, toward my bed. He reached down, and with one motion grabbed my sleeping bag and threw it open. There, in a tight ball at the bottom of the bed, was the boa!

Chapter Twenty

I did a quick double take. This was like some sort of strange miracle, or an optical illusion, or a hallucination or . . . a magic trick. The way Augie pulled back the cover to "reveal" the snake. It lay there, unmoving.

"Aren't you going to grab it?" Augie demanded.

"Yeah, of course." I went to reach for it and then stopped. "No, I'm not," I said, thinking it through a little more. "Hand me the burlap sack. It's there," I said, gesturing in the general direction of the pile on the floor. I didn't want to take my eyes off the snake even for a second, for fear it would somehow disappear— the reverse of Augie's magic trick.

I could hear Augie shuffling things around as he rummaged through the pile. Out of the very corner of my eye I could see him.

"Here it is!" he announced. He passed it over to me.

I took the bag and quickly started to roll the lip of it down.

"What do you want me to do?" Augie asked.

"Nothing," I said.

"Nothing?"

I nodded. "I'll take care of it."

There was no time to be timid or tentative or scared. I leaped on the bed and in one motion scooped the sleeping ball of snake up into my hands and into the bag. Before it could even react, I unrolled the bag and sealed the top with my hands, trapping the snake inside. It started to move around. Obviously it was awake and not happy about leaving its nice warm bed—*my* nice warm bed!

"That was amazing!" Augie said. "I bet the snake guy at Reptile World couldn't do it that good!"

"It was pretty good," I admitted, holding the bag tightly. It was like I hadn't had the time to worry.

"But what was really amazing," I continued, "was you finding the snake. That was really something! How did you know to look there?"

"I told you, I was thinking like a snake," Augie explained. "You said they liked hot places and then I remembered you telling me about how rattlesnakes sometimes climb into people's sleeping bags at night when it gets cold, and I figured a snake is a snake and . . . voila!"

"That was something," I said again.

Augie smiled and bowed from the waist. "Did you expect less?"

I started laughing. It wasn't just what he'd said but how incredibly relieved I felt.

I turned and suddenly caught sight of the clock. It

was twenty-five minutes to one—twenty-five minutes until the assembly began. "We have to get going. Maybe we can still make it."

"Doubtful," Augie said. "It normally takes twenty minutes when we move fast and we're not lugging fifty pounds of snake along with us."

"We'll just have to try. Come on!"

I rushed out of my room, carrying the sack awkwardly, lumbering down the stairs, trying hard not to bang the bag against anything.

"Can you grab my backpack as well as yours?" I yelled.

"Just leave it here."

"Our assignment on friendship is in there and it's due today."

Augie slung his pack onto his back and grabbed mine and put it over one shoulder. He hurried out the door and I followed, clicking the lock on and then slamming the door closed behind me. I took a step across the porch and then stopped, turned around quickly and jiggled the lock, just to make sure. I'd already had enough problems today with something getting *out* when it should have stayed in, to risk somebody getting *in* who should be staying out.

"It's locked . . . it's *always* locked!" Augie yelled from the sidewalk. "Hurry up!"

I jumped down the stairs and stumbled up the walk. It was going to be hard to move with any speed at all. There had to be a better way to carry the boa. I threw the sack over my shoulder. If it worked for Santa Claus, it could work for me. Of course, Santa usually had toys inside, not a snake. A snake that was writhing around—I could feel it against my back.

I moved as quickly as I could, trying to match the pace Augie was setting. I struggled along the whole first block. The bag was getting heavier and heavier, and I could feel my breath becoming more laboured.

"Do you think you can carry it for a while?" I panted.

"If I have to," Augie offered reluctantly.

"You do if we're gonna have any chance of getting there even just a little late."

I put down the bag and he handed me the two back-packs. They didn't seem that much lighter than the snake. Augie took the bag in both hands and held it in front of him, well away from his body. There was no way we'd be travelling very fast with him carrying it like that, but at least I'd get a rest. We started moving again. We made it down Silverthorn, passing Elyse's house—she must be going nuts waiting for us to arrive . . . wondering what we were doing. We turned onto St. Clair Avenue.

"What time is it?" Augie asked.

I looked at my watch. "Almost five minutes to one."

"We still might make it. Can you take the bag again?"

"Sure." We exchanged the backpacks for the snake. I slung the snake back over my shoulder.

"Let's cross here," Augie said, taking me by the arm and aiming me across the busy street as a streetcar rumbled by in the opposite direction. There was a gap in the traffic and we scurried halfway across, stopping at the yellow line. A couple of cars and a big truck rumbled past before we could cross the rest of the way.

"We're going to have to take the shortcut," Augie said. "We have to go through the alley and cut in the back way."

"The alley! We can't go into the alley! Let's just take the long way around and—"

"There isn't time for that."

"But what if we run into—"

"We won't run into anybody, it's after lunch—all the high school kids are back at their school. And even if we do, nothing will happen. Come on, it's not like they can take money off us that we don't have," Augie said as he turned down the alley.

I hesitated for just a second before following him. He was right. We didn't have much time and this would save us at least four or five minutes—minutes we needed.

"Right now, all the kids in the whole school are being shepherded into the auditorium," Augie said. "And every single person is waiting for us. In just a few minutes we'll be back stage, just hiding behind the curtain. And then Mr. Skully will call our names and we'll walk across the stage. And every eye in the whole place will be on us as we hand Mr. Johnston the snake. Are you nervous?"

"I am now," I admitted. Actually, I'd been so caught up in finding the snake and getting here for the assembly that I hadn't had time to be worried. Now I had time.

"Don't worry. I'll speak. All you have to do is hold the snake and—"

"And what?" I asked.

"We have company," Augie said, looking over his shoulder.

I glanced behind us. Three teenagers had suddenly materialized. Probably they'd stepped out from behind one of the garages that lined the alley. In the two seconds before I turned back around I could see that they not only outnumbered us, but also were older, at least by a few years, and bigger—not to mention a lot tougher looking than the two of us.

"What do we do?" I whispered.

"We keep walking . . . maybe just a little faster—we can outrun them if we have to."

Augie was right. We were two of the fastest people in the whole school—but carrying a sack full of snake?

"I don't know how fast I can run with the snake," I said.

"Look, they probably aren't going to bother us any—"

Augie stopped as he saw what I'd just seen. Two more teenagers—one of them Jimmie Saunders—

stepped out from some hidden space just up ahead of us. We were trapped!

"What do we do?" I asked. I felt panicked.

"Nothing," Augie said under his breath. "We keep walking. Maybe they don't even know each other, maybe they'll leave us alone, maybe—"

"Look what we got here," Jimmie called out.

"Two kids trespassing in our alley is what I think we have," a second kid answered.

"And look, they have on the same pants," Jimmie said. "They look sort of like identical dorks." He snickered and the rest joined in.

Augie and I stopped as they continued to come toward us.

"I'm going to try to talk my way out of this," Augie said quietly to me. "But if I can't talk us out, then you run when I give you the signal."

"What's the signal?" I whispered.

"I'm going to punch Jimmie in the face and jump on the second one blocking your way."

I gave him a stunned look . . . he couldn't be serious.

Jimmie and his friend stopped just a few feet in front of us. I could hear the other three just behind us. I took a quick look over my shoulder.

"Either of you two have any cigarettes?" one of them asked.

"Um, no . . . sorry . . . we don't smoke," I stuttered.

"But if we did we'd give them to you," Augie added.

"Isn't that nice of them," one of the others joked. "Willing to give us things. Maybe you got some money you'd like to give us so we can buy our own cigarettes?"

"We don't have any money on us," Augie said.

"That's too bad, cause this here is private property, and you can't just go walking on somebody's property without paying to pass."

"We could bring you money . . . tomorrow," Augie offered.

"Not interested in what you can bring tomorrow. What you got today?" one of the kids behind us said.

"Books, papers, you know, our school stuff," Augie said.

"What's in the sack?" one of them asked.

"Nothing!" I snapped.

"Looks like a pretty big nothing. Let me have a look," Jimmie said as he reached forward to take the bag.

"No, you can't see it!" I shouted as I pulled it away and staggered a few feet to the side. Jimmie looked shocked that I'd done what I did. He wasn't used to people not doing what he wanted.

"Don't give us a hard time, kid!" he threatened, and two of the others closed in on me. I backed into one of the garages. I thought about the smashed cages, the dead turtles, about the expression on Mr. Johnston's face when he told us Bogart was dead. Nobody—not even Jimmie—was going to hurt another snake!

"You can't have it!"

"I don't see who's going to stop us from taking it!" he said as he tried to grab the bag out of my hands.

I hung on, not letting him take it, refusing to let go. "It's for Mr. Johnston!"

Jimmie released his grip on the bag. "Mr. Johnston . . . the science teacher at Osler?"

"Yeah."

"You guys remember Mr. Johnston, don't you?" Jimmie said to the other kids.

"Of course," one of them said.

"Best teacher I ever had," another replied.

"Me too," Jimmie said, nodding. "He always treated me good. So what you got in the bag for Mr. Johnston?"

"It's . . . it's a snake."

"The new snake?" Jimmie asked.

"Um, yeah . . . it is . . . but how did you know?" I said.

"We all heard about what happened to Bogart and that some kids were collecting money to buy him a new snake. Are you the guys?"

"Yeah, me and Augie," I said. "We're giving it to him today, in an assembly that's supposed to take place right now. That's the only reason we cut through the alley. We didn't mean to trespass . . . we'll never do it again, honest."

"What time's the assembly?" Jimmie asked.

"It's supposed to start at one," I said.

"That's in, like, two minutes. You better get going."

"We can go?" Augie asked.

"Of course you can go. What did you think we were going to do, kill you?"

"No . . . it's just . . ."

"Get going, hurry!"

They moved out of the way to let us pass. We stumbled down the alley.

"HEY!"

I turned back around.

"Say hello to Mr. Johnston from Jimmie Saunders, and tell him he was the best teacher I ever had in my life!"

"Sure . . . of course!" Augie called back.

"And if you two ever want to take the alley again, and anybody bothers you, you just tell them you're friends with Jimmie. Understand?"

"Yeah, thanks!" Augie yelled back.

"Now hurry up or you'll be late!"

Chapter Twenty-One

Classes were moving through the halls toward the gym for the assembly. Kids and teachers turned and talked to us as we passed them. We mumbled short answers and greetings. We didn't have time to talk. We had to get to the door that led up to the stage, and do it without running into Mr. Johnston. A couple of people asked to have a look at the snake. We brushed them off. There wasn't time, but anyway, I was only planning on opening that bag once—just before I handed it to Mr. Johnston.

"Do you want me to carry the bag for a minute?" Augie said.

"I'm okay." Suddenly it didn't seem heavy. In fact, I had the strangest feeling throughout my whole body—almost like I was floating, my feet just brushing the floor. Besides, now that we were here and it was all really going to happen, I didn't want to take my hands off this snake until I put it directly in Mr. Johnston's hands.

Up ahead we could see Mr. Skully standing by the stage door.

"Cutting it a little tight, aren't you, gentlemen?" he asked.

"We didn't want to get here too early in case we ran into Mr. Johnston," Augie said, offering the perfect excuse.

"I was just getting ready to call home to find out where you two were," Mr. Skully said. "Now, here's what's going to happen at the assembly. Our principal will be addressing the entire school, talking about the break-in and how the theft and vandalism have had an effect on everybody. How troubling it has been to have our school violated. Then he's going to mention how some students worked very hard to help clean up the school. He's then going to call up Mr. Johnston and ask him to present certificates of appreciation to those students. Mr. Johnston will be calling the two of you up to the stage to receive your awards."

"We're getting awards?" I asked.

"Of course not," Augie said, answering for Mr. Skully. "That's just so we can all be up on stage together to give Mr. Johnston the snake."

"Exactly," Mr. Skully said. "When he calls your names, the two of you walk onto the stage with the snake."

"I have a little speech," Augie said. "Do you want to hear it?"

"I'm sure it will be fine." He paused. "Is the snake in the bag?"

"Yes," I said, holding it up with both hands.

"That's a big bag . . . just how big is the snake?"

"It's pretty big," I said.

"It's even bigger than Bogart was," Augie said. "We got a really good deal."

"Lovely."

"Do you want to see it?" Augie asked.

Mr. Skully shook his head. Judging from the look on his face, he *really* didn't want to see the snake.

"We don't have time. You two have to take your spot at the side of the stage."

He pulled at the door. It was locked. "I'll circle around, open it from the inside and let you in," Mr. Skully said.

"You nervous?" Augie asked me.

"Not as much as I thought I'd be."

"So standing in front of the whole school doesn't make you nervous?" he asked in disbelief.

"I'll be fine. I'm not giving a speech, and besides, I'm not the one who's fly isn't done up all the way."

Augie's eyes widened and then he reached down and pulled his up. "Stupid zipper keeps slipping down."

"Augie! Ricky!"

We turned around . . . it was Elyse!

"You two had me worried," she said. "I thought you weren't going to show."

"We were a little worried ourselves," I said.

"Yeah, something happened that we didn't quite see coming—we'll tell you later."

"So you're not usually late?" she asked.

"Hardly ever," Augie said.

"Good, because there's nothing worse than going to a dance late. You miss the first dance and —"

"Dance? What do you mean 'dance'?" Augie asked.

"The dance. This Friday. I was hoping we could go together," she said.

"You want me to take you to the dance?" Augie gasped.

"Not you . . . both of you. What do you think?"

I shrugged. "I wasn't planning on going."

"Of course he's going . . . we're both going. How about we pick you up around seven?"

"That would be great. And I hope you don't mind, but a friend of mine from my old school is visiting and she'll be coming with us."

"That would be no problem!" Augie exclaimed.

The stage door suddenly opened. Mr. Skully popped his head out and motioned for us to enter.

"Why don't you come in with us?" Augie said. "Best place to see everything is from the stage."

She shook her head. "It's you two that belong up there on stage, but I'll come and watch from the wings."

We walked through the door and up a small set of steps. The stage was just off to the side. It was deserted except for our principal and a couple of kids from the audio-visual club who were setting up two microphones in the middle of the stage. The kids waved to us as we followed Mr. Skully across the back of the stage. The curtain was closed, but it didn't block the sound of the crowd.

I suddenly had a rush of fear—bigger than in the alley just a few minutes ago—bigger than when I discovered the snake was gone. I had to fight the urge to simply hand Augie the bag and run away. The thought of standing in front of the whole school felt . . . Everybody would be staring at me. I reached down and checked *my* fly. At least that part of me was still okay.

"This is where you wait. Now remember, stay out of sight and wait for your cue. You'll be coming up on stage almost immediately after Mr. Johnston does. Break a leg!"

"What?" I asked.

"It's theatre talk," Elyse said. "It means good luck."

"Thanks," Augie said.

All at once I became aware that the noise from the kids had faded. The teachers must be quieting everybody down. It then got brighter where we stood, as the big curtain at the front was pulled back. Augie peeked around the corner.

"The place is packed," he said.

Of course, he wasn't telling me anything I didn't

already know, but my stomach still tightened another notch.

"Good afternoon, ladies and gentlemen," called out the voice of our principal, Mr. MacDonald.

I could tell by the metallic sound of his voice that he was using the microphone.

Augie leaned closed to me. "Bet you a dollar he uses the word *co-operation* before he introduces Mr. Johnston."

"No bet. He uses that word in every speech."

Elyse grinned. "He uses that word in every conversation. Shouldn't you get ready to pull the snake out?"

"Yeah, sure," I said. I put the bag on the ground and started to untie the knot. My hands were shaking slightly and the knot seemed to be a lot snugger than I remembered tying it. It must have tightened up during the walk.

"I'd now like to ask Mr. Johnston to come forward to present the first awards," our principal announced.

"Hurry up!" Augie said as the crowd clapped for Mr. Johnston.

"I'm trying, I'm trying," I said, my fingers fumbling with the burlap knot. I pulled at it desperately as I heard Mr. Johnston start to talk. Maybe I could just hand him the sack and let him open it in front of— The knot slipped open!

"These were very difficult times for all of us," Mr.

Johnston said. "Maybe for me, more than for other people." He paused, and I could feel the emotions of his words sink into my skull. It had been awful.

"But some students helped to undo the damage. They worked to try to make things right."

I opened up the bag and looked inside. The snake was coiled in a big ball. I thrust in my hand and fumbled around, trying to grab it just behind the head. It came to life and started to twirl and jerk around. The last thing I wanted was for its head to grab me—for it to sink its fangs into my hand.

"And the first two students I'd like to acknowledge are Ricky and Augie. Could they please come up onto the stage to accept their awards!" Mr. Johnston called out.

"Come on," Augie said.

"I'm trying!" Finally I grabbed the boa by the head. With my other hand I reached farther into the bag and grabbed the rest of the snake, pulling it free of the bag, which then dropped to the floor. Elyse pulled back the curtain to let us walk onto the stage.

"Let's go," Augie said, as the crowd started to clap.

I followed Augie. As I stepped onto the stage I heard first a gasp, and then total silence. Nobody was expecting a snake this big. Then somebody called out, and then somebody else and then everybody started to clap and cheer. I didn't dare look out at the crowd. Instead I looked straight ahead, straight at Mr. Johnston. His eyes grew large and his mouth dropped open. He looked completely and utterly amazed.

Augie stepped to one of the microphones and then raised his hands in the air to quiet the crowd. They didn't want to be quieted, and kept on cheering for a few more seconds.

"Mr. Johnston, we have to apologize for tricking you, but we wanted this to be a surprise. All of us were pretty upset about what happened to Bogart, and Ricky had an idea about how to help make it up to you. Almost everybody in the whole school chipped in money to buy you another boa constrictor, and we'd like to present you with that snake." Augie turned to me. "Ricky."

"Unbelievable." Mr. Johnston gasped. "Unbelievable."

I stepped forward, reached out and handed Mr. Johnston the snake. He gently took it from my hands. As I released my grip, it felt like a gigantic weight had been lifted from my shoulders.

"I . . . I don't know what to say," Mr. Johnston stammered.

"You don't have to say anything," I said. "It was just something we wanted to do."

I looked up at Mr. Johnston standing there, holding the snake, and for the second time in my life, I saw a teacher cry.

Author's Note

I guess every book is special to its author. To me this book is even more special. Ricky isn't just about things I've imagined but things I've lived. It is based on my life, my friendship with Augie and an experience we shared when we were grade eight students at Osler Senior Public School in Toronto. Writing this book helped me to gain a better understanding of where I came from and who I became. It brought back long-forgotten memories and helped to rekindle an old friendship. It allowed me to find a former teacher and say "thank you" for what he shared.

I'm often asked by children, "Which is your favourite book that you've written?" I usually answer that my favourite is the book I'm writing right now. That may still be true, but I definitely know my second favourite book, and know the place it has in my heart.

I'd like to tell you what happened to the characters you got to know through this book. Mr. Grant Johnston continued to teach with the Toronto Board of Education before he and his wife changed boards, moving to the city of Peterborough, where they raised their family and where he taught until his retirement. He continues his many interests: photography, videography, the outdoors, and spending time with his family. Mr. Johnston raised the boa constrictor he was given for seven years before he finally donated it to the Metropolitan Toronto Zoo. Mr. Johnston was a role model and an inspiration to me when I was young. Having renewed contact, he remains both.

Augie Levy became known as Aaron Levy. He spent time in high school perfecting his imitations and stand-up comedy. He finally settled down and opened his own store, Levy's Discount Designer Clothing, on St. Clair Avenue West in Toronto—not far from Osler. Augie says that "the store is now his stage." He's married and has six children—five girls and then, finally, a boy. Augie, despite the change in name to Aaron, remains Augie. He is spirited, alive and lives life large, sharing his unique view of the world with all those fortunate enough to know him. Drop into his store sometime—maybe he'll give you a deal.

Osler Senior Public School is a real school in Toronto and is located on Osler Avenue, although it is now known as Carlton Village Public School.

Ricky became known as Rick and then finally Eric Walters—the name I was given at birth. I married and had three wonderful children, Christina, Nicholas and Julia. I became a social worker, an elementary school teacher and, eventually a writer of books for children and young adults. I live happily in Mississauga, but still, whenever I find myself anywhere near the old neighbourhood, I go back and remember.